Booked Up

A Village Library Mystery, Volume 10

Elizabeth Craig

Published by Elizabeth Spann Craig, 2024.

BOOKED UP

First edition. January 31, 2024.

Written by Elizabeth Craig.

Chapter One

I was just stepping off the treadmill when my boyfriend, Grayson, walked over from the other side of the gym.

"So, what do you think of this place?" he asked with a cheerful grin. "Do we approve?"

I said wryly, "I think the question is more 'do *you* approve? You're the one who's contemplating a gym membership here."

I took a small towel to wipe down the treadmill, in case of any sweaty spattering. There was plenty of cause for there to be spattering. While Grayson had taken a tour of the gym, I'd tried out the various equipment here. Now he was still delightfully clean in his jeans and button-down shirt. He had no perspiration dripping from his light-brown hair like I did from my black hair. Grayson said, "Well, so far, it seems pretty good."

"Yeah, I think so, too. I liked the amount of equipment the gym has. It's nice not to have to wait too long for the stair-climber or the weights."

Grayson nodded. "It makes a difference. Let's try out the café they have here."

"No way. They have a *café* in the gym?"

Grayson nodded. "According to the tour that I got, yes. I think smoothies were mentioned a lot, though. I'm not sure how much solid food they have there."

"I'm not sure how much solid food I even need after that workout. But a smoothie sounds pretty good."

We wandered into the café, a sunny room with brightly painted walls. It turned out they offered some breakfast sandwiches, but I stuck with a berry smoothie. Grayson got some sort of Uber-healthy green drink. We settled into a booth.

"So?" I asked. "What did you make of your tour?" Grayson had brought me along as a guest today. I was trying to work in more exercising, realizing I spent a good deal of time sitting. The library was actually a fairly active job, between hopping up to help patrons find books and other materials and wrangling the evil copier we had. But I still felt I needed more sustained cardio exercise and my once-a-week jogs weren't really cutting it.

"I liked it," said Grayson. "It doesn't seem super-crowded. The people who are here don't look like bodybuilder types or anything, so it's not very intimidating being here. It seems like they offer a variety of exercise machines, and the place is spotless." He paused. "I hope it's okay, but I got a family membership."

He looked so worried that I couldn't help but smile. "This, despite the fact that you don't have any local family?"

"Yeah." He stirred his green drink, not meeting my eyes. "I hope you don't mind, but I thought I could get it for the both of us. I'm paying for it, of course."

At one point, there would be no "of course" about it. Grayson and I had always been fairly equal partners in terms of clipping coupons, shopping sales, and eating packed lunches. But when Grayson's wealthy Charleston uncle passed away, he left Grayson a surprise legacy. Grayson has still been trying to come to terms with it all. It's not quite a rags-to-riches story, but it's not far off the mark, either. We skirted the issue of money most days, which made both of us feel less awkward. This was the first time he'd offered to pay for anything more than the occasional dinner out.

Before I could say anything, Grayson continued in a rush. "I know. It was really presumptuous of me. You can totally get me to cancel it. But the thing was, it wasn't that much more expensive than an individual membership. Plus, I'll feel a lot more motivated if you come with me. Sort of like the buddy system. Maybe we can even make a couple fitness goal."

He looked anxiously up at me through his long lashes. I sighed, shaking my head. I never had the ability to stay irritated with Grayson, even if I tried. "Hey, it's a nice thing to do."

"I should have checked with you first."

"Yes, you should have." I considered the offer. "But I totally agree that I'd feel more motivated about coming if you and I did it together. If I didn't want to get up early and exercise one day, knowing you were here waiting for me would make me push through it. And I definitely can't afford a gym membership. There's just no question about that. Plus, I don't have room in my house for weights or a treadmill or anything. So, sure. Thank you." I hoped I didn't sound ungrateful. Our relationship and how we were both contributing to it seemed like it was balancing nicely.

Grayson blew out a relieved sigh, clearly glad to put that part of the conversation behind him. "Okay, good. So do *you* like this place? What did you make of it? I know you said you liked the fact that there was plenty of equipment there. You thought the rest of it was okay?"

"I thought it was great. I'm kind of sorry I decided not to go on the tour with you. I walked around a little, though, and saw the sauna, the weight room, and the swimming pool. It's actually a really nice set-up for a town this size."

Grayson said eagerly, "I thought so, too. I was going to see if they wanted to advertise in the newspaper. I had no idea all the stuff they had available over here. If they advertise, they can really get the word out." He slid a brochure across the table to me. "Here's their exercise class schedule. Maybe we can consider doing one of those, too."

I glanced over the list. They had all sorts of offerings, from gentle yoga to hard-core cycling. "Sure, we can give one or two of them a go. I'm going to want to start out with the beginner stuff to make sure I know what I'm doing first. I've never done any group exercise classes."

"Good idea." Grayson was already thinking ahead. "I know things can be tough with our schedules. What do you think will work better: early mornings or after work?"

"Maybe a combination of them. And maybe I can squeeze in a little at lunch, although I couldn't get too sweaty. Maybe weight resistance or something." I smiled at him. "However we work it out, it's got to be better than what we're doing right now."

We switched to talking about other subjects then. Grayson had been working on some profiles for the newspaper and talked a little about some people he thought he might focus on down the road.

"There's this local artist who creates incredible sculptures out of recycled materials. I'm sure people will want to hear her story."

"That sounds really cool. What kinds of sculptures are we talking about?

Grayson said, "She mostly uses old car parts and scrap metal from the junkyard, turning them into these amazingly intricate works of art. She emailed me a picture of one of them." He scrolled through his phone and showed me a picture of an owl she'd made. It had a steampunk look about it, but also, strangely, as if it could take off and fly at any moment."

"That's incredible. Part of me has always wished I could be an artist. You can say so much with a piece like this."

Grayson said, "A picture's worth a thousand words? But you love your books so much."

"True. I guess visual art just speaks in a different way." I glanced at my watch. "I've still got plenty of time, but we should probably start heading toward the car. I'll need to rinse off before going to work."

I was working a morning shift at the library. My favorite shifts were early in the morning because I loved going in first thing. The gym opened at five o'clock in the morning, which meant Grayson and I wouldn't have a problem fitting in exercise before work. We'd arrived there at six and it was now a couple of minutes after seven.

We climbed into Grayson's car, and he set off slowly down the street as we continued chatting with each other. I said, "There's no way I can convince Zelda to go to the gym, but I'm wondering if I can convince her to stop chain-smoking. Her cough has gotten really nasty lately."

Grayson gave me a wry grin. "Is that because you're deeply concerned about Zelda? Or because her horrible cough is driving you nuts at the library?"

Zelda was a library volunteer and the president of our homeowner's association. Although she could certainly be helpful, she was also a handful.

"A little of both," I admitted. "I'll have to see if I can get my hands on some library resources to send her home with on quitting smoking."

I was looking out the passenger window, mulling over Zelda's many issues, when I spotted Linus, one of the library's regular patrons, tugging hard at his dog's leash. Ivy was usually a sweet girl and very obedient. It looked as if Linus was struggling to control her.

"Hey, that's Linus," I blurted out. "Can you find a spot to pull over?"

Grayson quickly parallel parked on the side of the road, and we both hopped out of the car. "Linus?" I called.

The older man turned around, looking relieved. As usual, he was wearing suit pants and a button-down shirt with a tie. "Hi, you two. Do you mind lending me a hand? I don't know what's gotten into Ivy. She's never like this."

Grayson quickly took Ivy's leash and led her gently but firmly back onto the sidewalk and away from a business's driveway.

The dog still seemed agitated and as if she wanted to run over to investigate whatever she'd been so interested in. I said, "Has she been like this for a while?"

"No, just right here. The rest of the walk really went fine. But when we got up here, I thought she was going to pull the leash away and run off." Linus sounded panicked at the concept. He had grown very close to the former stray. It was almost as if she'd picked her owner—she'd been discovered on the library property, and Linus had immediately been smitten.

"How about if we cut her walk short today?" asked Grayson. "You and she can hop in the car, and I can drive you both home. Maybe she just needs some downtime today."

I thought Linus was going to refuse the help since he was always reluctant to put anyone out. It was a testament to how worried he'd been about controlling Ivy that he quickly said, "That's very kind of you. I think that sounds like a good idea."

There was something so odd about Ivy's change of behavior that it gave me pause. "I'll join you in just a second. I just wanted to check something really quick."

"Want me to come with you?" asked Grayson, suddenly sounding concerned. It must have occurred to him, too, that there must be something out of the ordinary out there to make Ivy act so very out of character.

I shook my head. "I'll just be a second."

I walked toward the business driveway Ivy had been pulling toward. The business was a medical clinic, which had been around forever. Long enough that a thick hedge lined the front entrance of the property, obscuring some of the building and grounds from view. I took a quick glance toward the clinic. The exterior of the medical practice was a quaint, one-story structure painted a neutral cream. The front door was an inviting shade of red under a wooden overhang. I walked down the driveway a few moments and stopped short. There was a man lying on the ground, a stethoscope around his neck, and a thick medical reference book on the ground next to him.

Chapter Two

I quickly backed up. I recognized the man as Victor Sullivan, a doctor at the practice.

"Everything okay?" called Grayson from the car.

I shook my head. "Can you call the police?"

Without asking questions, Grayson dug out his phone. I walked carefully back to the body. Victor certainly seemed to be dead. The stethoscope wasn't dangling around his neck in a professional manner; it appeared to have been used to strangle him. His eyes were wide open. His keys, perhaps to the office, were next to his hand. Victor was in his late-fifties with blond hair with a few streaks of gray throughout. His wire glasses were slightly askew.

I put a cautious couple of fingers on his neck, checking for a pulse. There wasn't one. His skin was still warm, so he couldn't have been lying there very long.

I walked back to the car, striding up to the driver's side window. Grayson, now off the phone, gave me a quizzical look as a siren sounded in the background.

"What's happened?" he asked.

Linus was sitting in the backseat with Ivy and rolled his window down, too. I could see Ivy leaning against Linus as he stroked her in an attempt to calm her down. Her eyes were still wide, though, and she seemed agitated.

"I'm afraid that the reason Ivy was so determined to go into that medical practice was because there was a body there," I said. "It's one of the doctors who works at the clinic. I recognized him from around town, although I don't know him well." I paused. "It looked like he was murdered."

Ivy whined again from the backseat as the siren grew closer. Her sweet face looked concerned as she peered out the window.

Grayson said, "Linus, is it okay if we wait to talk to Burton first before I drop you back at your house? I'm sure he's going to want to ask us questions."

"Of course it is. We were first on the scene, after all. I don't have anything going on at home that I need to get back to. Although I have to admit to feeling bad about being so incurious about what was keeping Ivy from continuing on her walk," said Linus wryly. "I didn't even try to see what she was so interested in. What a terrible thing to happen."

Burton Edison was the local police chief and friend of mine. And he was, I was sure, about to have an unexpectedly challenging day.

Burton was there in just a minute. He was a heavyset, middle-aged man, tall and solid, with kind eyes and a receding hairline. He spotted us, waved, took a quick look behind the hedge and checked the body, then strung up crime scene tape. A deputy was there with him and stood by the tape to ensure no one walked in and contaminated the scene.

Burton shook his head as he walked up to me. "Good morning, Ann. Not what you were expecting at the start of your day, was it? Were you on your way in for an appointment at the doctor's office?"

I shook my head. "Grayson and I were working out together at the gym. We pulled over when we saw Linus struggling with his dog. You remember Linus, my friend from the library?"

Burton nodded. He'd dated my coworker, Luna, for a while, and Linus was one of Luna's and my favorites. He lifted his eyebrows. "I'm guessing Linus's dog found the body."

"He and Ivy didn't get that far. But she definitely knew something was wrong over there. Ivy is usually a really sweet girl. The fact she wasn't listening to Linus and was pulling at the leash was totally out of character. Grayson pulled the car over, we helped Linus get Ivy into the vehicle, and then I walked over to see what Ivy was so interested in."

Burton nodded. "Got it. And you know who the victim is? I haven't been in town long enough to recognize everybody."

"It's murder, of course, isn't it?" I asked.

Burton gave another curt nod. "Sure looks that way."

I said, "He's Victor Sullivan, a primary care doctor. His death is probably going to really have tongues wagging. He's been practicing for a while and knows lots of people here."

Burton looked glum. "Great. There's nothing like a high-profile case to make life stressful. Good thing I've got the state police coming in to give me a hand." He glanced over at the car where Grayson, Linus, and Ivy still sat. "Let me speak with them real quick so you can be on your way. You're working this morning?"

"Yes. I'll be running a little late." I pulled my phone out to send a quick text to Wilson, the library director, to let him know.

While Burton was speaking with Grayson and Linus, a woman in her early-fifties walked up to me. She had sharp features, piercing blue eyes, and brown hair pulled back in a tidy bun. She looked familiar, but I couldn't place her name.

"What's going on?" she asked me briskly, gesturing toward the police and the crime scene tape.

"There's been an incident," I said quietly.

"I gathered that," she answered in rather an acerbic voice. "And I'm not asking from mere idle interest. That's my workplace. I'm Paige Lee, a doctor at the clinic."

"Ann Beckett," I said. I motioned for Burton to come over. If Dr. Lee was one of Victor Sullivan's coworkers, it would be better if Burton delivered the news.

Burton came over and introduced himself. Dr. Lee impatiently identified herself again. "What has happened?" she asked again. "Was there a break-in? People don't seem to realize that we don't have a huge stash of drugs on the premises."

Burton said, "I'm afraid it's something a bit more serious than theft. It looks as if one of your colleagues has died."

Dr. Lee knit her brows together. She looked surprised and confused, but not particularly upset. "One of my colleagues? Who was it?"

"Preliminary identification indicates he's Victor Sullivan."

Dr. Lee drew in a hissing breath. "Victor? Did he suffer a heart attack?"

Burton said carefully, "We're going to be treating his death as suspicious."

She took a step backward. "No. Murder? That's impossible."

Burton took out a small notebook. "As a formality, I need to ask everyone Dr. Sullivan worked with to tell me where they were this morning."

Dr. Lee frowned. "This morning? Is that when Victor died? I was at home, of course, getting ready for work. If you're looking for an alibi, however, I'm afraid I'm not going to be able to provide one. I'm not married, and I live alone. If Simone, my cat, could speak for me, I'd have a great alibi, but I doubt she'll be able to comply."

Burton seemed to wait for a bit more detail in terms of Dr. Lee's movements for the morning. She pressed her lips into a thin line before saying, "I got up for the day around six o'clock. Then I got ready, fed the cat, drank my coffee, and checked the news online. After that, I watered my houseplants and the plants on my front porch." She gestured to her laptop bag. "I gathered my things together and drove over here."

Burton made a few more notes. "Thanks for clarifying that. Could you speak a little as to your relationship with Victor Sullivan?"

Dr. Lee pressed her lips together. Then she said in a clipped, reserved voice, "I didn't have a 'relationship' with Victor. We were colleagues, plain and simple. Working with Victor was just fine. We collaborated on many cases, and he was a competent physician. Our interactions were strictly within the professional realm. Victor was dedicated to his work, and our discussions primarily revolved around patient care and medical matters. It's important to maintain a professional atmosphere in a healthcare setting, and that's precisely what we did."

"Were you close at all outside of work? Did you attend social functions together? Go to a restaurant? Coffee? Anything like that?"

Dr. Lee shook her head. "Not at all. We kept our professional and personal lives completely separate."

"Could you tell me more about what Victor was like as a person? I wasn't acquainted with him," said Burton.

Dr. Lee appeared to consider this. She carefully said, "He was very popular with his patients." She glanced at me. "You've been around town for a while, I know. You've probably heard everyone singing his praises." There was a touch of bitterness in her voice.

I nodded. "I know he was a patient favorite." I had the feeling that Dr. Lee might be an excellent doctor, but that her bedside manner could use a little work. She seemed both remote and crisply disinterested at the same time. I wondered if she had the same approach to patients in exam rooms.

Burton said, "No angry patients, then? No threats at the workplace? No one lost their parent and blamed Victor for malpractice?"

Dr. Lee gave a decisive shake of her head. "Nothing like that, at least that I'm aware of. They all seemed to think Victor was wonderful."

"What about Victor Sullivan's relationship with his coworkers and staff? Are you the only other physician in the practice?"

Dr. Lee said, "There's a medical student who's also currently working with us. He's on one of his clinical rotations for med school. That's it, in terms of providers." She frowned. "It's actually rather odd that our student isn't here yet. He's ordinarily something of an early bird. I suppose he either overslept or has been delayed on the highway. He commutes from Charlotte, but Kyle is still frequently here before I arrive."

Burton nodded, jotting down another note. "I'd like to hear more about your opinion of Dr. Sullivan, personally. What did you make of him? You must have known him fairly well, being the only other full-time provider at the practice. What can you tell me about him? Background information on the doctor will help my team figure out what happened to him."

A cautious look appeared on Dr. Lee's face. I had the feeling that she might not fully disclose what her feelings were about her coworker. Considering she was speaking to a police chief at a murder scene, however, it seemed pretty prudent to me.

She said in a halting voice, "He was an excellent doctor. He attended Duke University for medical school, specializing in internal medicine. He contributed significantly to medical research in his spare time, authoring numerous papers in reputable journals. Victor cared deeply about his patients and had many years of experience treating them."

Burton smiled at her, apparently to put her more at ease. But it appeared Dr. Lee wasn't going to relax, at least not around the police chief. She stood stiffly, her body tense. Burton said genially, "I'm sure I can find his resume online. What I'm more interested in is what he was like as a person."

"Unfortunately, considering we were colleagues, I'm better-positioned to speak on what he was like as a physician. Maybe you can draw some conclusions about his personality from his professional work." Dr. Lee thought for a moment, as if reflecting on Victor's professional habits. "He took a great deal of time with his patients. Victor wasn't one to run on time during the day. His patients knew to come to the office with a book or to download shows on their phones." There was a slightly irritated note in her voice. I got the impression that when Victor ran behind schedule, it inconvenienced her, too.

Burton picked up on the note, too. "You don't work the same way?"

Dr. Lee said, "I don't. I like to run on a particular timetable. I dislike keeping patients waiting since I feel their time is valuable. Sometimes they need to get back to their jobs or pick up their children from school. There are any number of reasons why it's preferable to keep the clinic running on time. But that was Victor's business. I prefer to do things my way."

"And Victor's personality?" pushed Burton. For him to keep pushing for it, he must be thinking Dr. Lee was being less than forthcoming.

Dr. Lee shrugged a thin shoulder. "Great with patients, but exacting with staff. He wanted our receptionist to answer calls quickly and always be cheerful and warm on the phone. He expected the nurses to perform well and be pleasant. He always pushed that the patients came first. If the receptionist and nurses didn't perform to his expectations, he could react angrily with them. We've lost some good staff through the years for that reason."

"You mentioned he was exacting with his staff. Did that include the medical student? And yourself?"

A flash of irritation crossed Dr. Lee's features. "I think Victor knew better than to be exacting with me. We were peers. Yes, we approached various tasks differently, but we were both successful in our own ways." She paused. "As for Kyle, our student? Yes, Victor could be tough on him. But that's what a clinical rotation is all about, isn't it?"

Burton's face indicated he had no idea. He said, "So the two of them might have had a challenging relationship."

"That's probably fair to say. I don't think it was difficult for Victor, but Kyle was likely affected by it. He's a very confident young student."

"Confident? Or cocky?" asked Burton.

Dr. Lee pressed her lips together before saying, "Maybe a bit of both. Kyle told me he didn't care for the way Victor was addressing him. Victor didn't feel Kyle was deferential enough to the patients. He thought Kyle came off as condescending or patronizing."

"How did Kyle react to that criticism?"

"Poorly," said Dr. Lee. "Kyle is used to getting excellent grades at med school and enthusiastic reviews on his rotations by his supervising physicians. So far, he'd breezed through his rotations. He was one of those young people who could be a little arrogant. I got the impression that Kyle wasn't excited about going through a primary care rotation. However, that's one of the rotations that's a staple for medical schools and is always required."

"You don't think he wants to be a primary care doctor?" asked Burton, still jotting down background notes.

"I know he doesn't. He plans on going into plastic surgery, I believe. I suspect he thought wading through a primary care rotation was a waste of his time. Victor, of course, considered primary care to be a vital rotation for every student. I could hear Victor in his office telling Kyle off about his attitude. He told Kyle that primary care was the foundation of holistic patient care. That we focused on preventative medicine, allowing doctors to identify and address health issues before they spiraled out of control."

Burton asked, "How did Kyle handle these little lectures he was getting in Victor's office?"

"Not particularly well. Kyle didn't enjoy being lectured to. He ranted to me about it. He thought Victor was too traditional, too focused on the old ways of practicing medicine. Kyle was all about modern medical innovations. He thought Victor didn't stay updated with the latest in medical technology."

"Was that true?" asked Burton.

"Perhaps. I know Victor read medical journals, but he was always more interested in his patients' symptoms and their medical histories than he was in technology. Kyle, on the other hand, thought the future of medicine lay with a more modern, cutting-edge approach. He's a kid, after all. He has a certain idealism about the future of healthcare, centered on innovation."

Burton scribbled down more notes. "And this obviously was causing friction between them."

"If you're asking me if I thought Kyle might lose it one day and murder Victor, the answer is no. I'd be shocked to hear that was the case. Was there friction, as you put it? Yes. But that was mostly because of a generation gap. Victor valued the fundamentals of medicine: doctor-patient relationships, and a deep knowledge of patient history. Kyle was eager for change and was excited about pushing the boundaries of what medicine could achieve. I believe that's why he was so interested in plastic surgery."

Dr. Lee seemed to be lost in thought for a few moments. Burton stayed quiet to let her.

"I know I said all Victor's patients loved him," she finally said slowly. "And, for the most part, that was true. But there's one patient who has been angry with Victor. Quite publicly angry, and for some time. This person just came to mind."

"Which patient is that?" Burton poised his pencil over the notepad.

Dr. Lee shook her head. "That's information I can't disclose without a warrant. I have HIPPA to consider, after all. However, this particular patient has made many public statements against Victor before, so it may be a matter of public record if you'd like to dig for that."

I immediately knew the patient she was talking about. She'd been nothing but overt about her anger over Victor Sullivan. Veronica was a patron of mine and had gotten me to help her complete some research. But because the library also believed in privacy, I decided not to say anything to Burton just yet. It was something I could follow up on privately.

"Now, if you'll excuse me, I need to contact the rest of the staff to fill them in. I'm assuming the clinic will need to be closed for the day?"

Burton gave a quick nod. "We have a forensic team on the way, but it's going to take some time. I wouldn't expect to open until tomorrow morning at the earliest."

"Then we'll need to reschedule today's appointments." Dr. Lee looked grim. "Excuse me while I get on with my phone calls."

Chapter Three

Burton watched a moment as the doctor walked away, her shoulders squared. He shook his head briefly, then walked closer to Grayson's car. "Thanks for waiting. I think I've got all the information I need from all of you for now. I know where to find you if I need anything else."

I climbed into the front seat of the car, and Grayson started driving away. Linus said in an anxious tone, "Ann, you shouldn't have had to find that body. I'm sorry. I was so focused on Ivy's unusual behavior that I didn't even think to try to learn what she was trying to pull me toward."

"Don't worry at all about that. The important thing is that the police know about the murder now and are starting their investigation." I looked back in the backseat and saw Ivy smiling a doggy grin at me. It made me smile back. "And that Ivy seems to be back to normal again."

Grayson said, "I guess my day is heading in a totally unexpected direction now. I'll be ditching my other work to focus on writing this story." He paused. "Ann, do you know who the victim was? I know you said it was one of the doctors at the practice."

Linus cleared his throat. "I'd like to know that, too. That clinic is where I go for my primary care."

I said slowly, "It's Victor Sullivan. Was he your doctor, Linus?"

There was a pause before Linus said quietly, "I'm afraid so."

"I'm so sorry, Linus. I know all his patients thought very highly of him."

Linus said, "Dr. Sullivan was pretty rare in the medical field. At least, he was in my limited experience. He was the kind of doctor who would really listen to you. He didn't look at his computer screen or type while you were telling him about your aches and pains. He'd look me in the eye with concern, then ask me questions. He'd take as long as needed in the exam room with you. I never got the feeling that I was being rushed out of there." He sighed. "I suppose I'll have to start seeing Dr. Lee now."

"You're not as fond of Dr. Lee?" I asked.

"From everything I can tell, she's an incredibly professional and successful physician. It's unfair for me to compare her with Dr. Sullivan. But she has this very brusque manner and a habit of looking at her watch when I'm speaking to her." He gave a wry chuckle. "Let's just say that I don't get the warm fuzzies from her the way I did for Dr. Sullivan. But times change, and we have to change with them." He paused. "I wonder if Dr. Lee will even be able to handle all of Dr. Sullivan's patients, or if I'll have to find another practice."

Grayson and I tried to encourage Linus, telling him it would all work out. Soon Grayson pulled up to Linus's modest brick house, not far from the library. He carefully climbed out of the backseat, Ivy in tow. "Thanks so much, Grayson. Ann, I'll see you at the library later on?"

"I'll be there," I said with a smile. "Just have to get cleaned up first."

We waved at Linus, and he walked away toward his front door with Ivy leading the way and now, thankfully, much calmer.

Grayson's mind was clearly already focused on the article he was going to write as he drove the short distance to my cottage. "It sounds like Victor Sullivan was an important figure in town. This is going to be a big story, isn't it?"

"That's what I was telling Burton. It's going to be a high-profile case. It will be hard for a lot of folks in town to believe that their doctor met a violent end in Whitby."

Grayson said, "Can you fill me in a little on what you saw? Of course I can't use it in the paper—Burton would kill me if I disclosed something from the crime scene that the cops wanted to keep quiet. But I'd like some background on what happened, just for my own benefit."

I took a deep breath, going back to the scene in my head. Grayson said quickly, "Sorry, Ann. That was insensitive of me. You don't want to relive that."

"No," I said slowly. "It's really fine. I think it will help me work things out in my mind if I replay it." I considered what I'd seen. "Of course, the first thing I wanted to do was to check Victor for a pulse. After that, I took a quick look at everything around him. It looked like he'd been hit over the head with a heavy medical reference book—there was blood pooling around his head. But Grayson, he'd also been strangled by his stethoscope."

Grayson pulled into my driveway and stopped the car. "That's awful," he said in a grim voice.

"It was. It looked like somebody just used whatever they had around them to kill him. Maybe that indicates that the crime was spur of the moment? That someone lashed out at him rashly?"

Grayson said, "Maybe. But if that's the case, isn't it weird that they killed him when he was going into work? It must have been pretty early in the morning. That doesn't sound like something that wasn't planned." He frowned. "I'm just guessing he was going into work. Do you think he was killed last night, instead, when he was heading back home?"

I shook my head. "His skin was still warm when I was searching for a pulse. Plus, he had keys near his hand, like he'd been getting his keys out to open the office door. You're probably right—the killer was waiting for him. He must have either been watching Victor or was familiar enough with his routine that he knew when he'd be coming into work."

"That information seems to point to a coworker, doesn't it?"

I said, "Maybe. You saw I spoke with Paige Lee. She's the other doctor in the practice."

Grayson said wryly, "It sounded like Linus wasn't too impressed with her."

"Well, I think she's probably great at her job, but doesn't have the bedside manner that Victor had. She came across pretty cold when Burton was talking with her, but then she'd just had a shock. Maybe she was just trying to wall herself off from her feelings so she could process them."

Grayson asked, "Do you know Dr. Lee?"

"I've seen her around town before, but I've never met her." I thought for a second. "She said that Victor wasn't as kind and generous to his staff as he was to his patients. Dr. Lee was talking about how he was with the nurses and the medical student who's there, but it made me wonder what her relationship with Victor was really like," I said.

"Did Burton ask her?"

"He did. She kind of clammed up," I said. "She basically said that they had a professional relationship, and that was it. They didn't meet outside of work or consider themselves friends outside of the office."

Grayson said, "Got it. Maybe I can call her and get a quote for the paper. She wasn't too upset?"

I considered this. "You know, it was really tough to read her. I got the impression she was surprised at Victor's death, but that she seemed to take it in stride. No, she didn't seem upset at all. She was very focused by the end of the interview on canceling patient appointments and informing the staff that the clinic would be closed for the day. But again, she might have been trying to process his death in her own way."

Grayson looked at his watch and grimaced. "Sorry. I'm keeping you from getting cleaned up and heading in to work." He glanced over at my house and grinned. "There's somebody who would like you to get him to the library as soon as possible."

I followed his gaze and saw my orange and white cat Fitz, looking inquisitively at me from the window. A sunbeam illuminated him as he watched me. It put a happy smile cross my face. I needed a cuddle, and Fitz was great for giving them.

Grayson was also wonderful at giving them. He reached over to pull me into a hug. I pulled back, protesting, "I'm all gross and sweaty, Grayson!"

"I don't care." He buried his face in my dark hair, and I felt some of the stress seep out of me. He pulled back and looked solemnly at me. "Call me today if you need me. Anytime. Are you sure you don't want to call out sick from work?"

I shook my head. "No, it'll be better for me to be at the library. You know that's my happy place. Anyway, keeping busy helps keep me from dwelling on it."

"Do you need me to run a lunch by later?"

I shook my head again. "No, thanks. I was actually super-organized last night and put together a pasta salad for lunch today. I just have to toss the container in my lunchbox." I hopped out of the car with more energy than I was feeling. "I'll talk to you later. Good luck writing your story."

Thirty minutes later, I was clean, wearing something professional-looking, and heading to the library with my lunch and Fitz in tow. Fitz seemed to have picked up on the fact something was wrong and was casting me sorrowful looks from his crate. When I hit a stoplight, I reached out and rubbed him on his little nose. He purred back at me.

The library was in full swing when I arrived. There was a large group of moms with toddlers who must have just left storytime. They'd converged at the circulation desk with gobs of board books and picture books and the moms were happily chatting with each other as they waited. The computer room was full of patrons working at the desktops, and the stacks seemed to be alive with browsers. It always made me happy to see so many people there, even if it meant a busier day.

I walked over to Wilson's office. He was the library director and the person I'd called to say I'd be late. Wilson was a big fan of punctuality, and I knew from personal experience it was much better to call in saying I'd be late than to just show up behind schedule. He was frowning at his computer, his prematurely white hair framing his face. His rimless glasses gave him something of a scholarly look, and he wore one of his omnipresent suits.

"Ann," he said as I walked in. "Everything okay?"

I filled him in quickly, having the feeling that I was going to be telling my story a lot today. Luna, my friend and coworker, was definitely going to want to hear it. As I told Wilson what happened, his frown deepened. "Oh no," he said. "Victor was my doctor, too." He gave a deep sigh. "What a mess."

I nodded. "Sorry about Victor's death. I know he was a great doctor."

"He was indeed." Wilson leaned back in his chair, thoughtfully. "I remember once I was having a very uncomfortable evening with some sort of nagging pain. It's the sort of thing where your imagination can blow it up into something much bigger than it actually is."

"Weird how those kinds of problems always seem to happen after office hours," I said. "Or over holidays."

"Precisely. After becoming even more uncomfortable, I called the office. I felt so incredibly miserable, and I realized I would not be sleeping at all. I knew no one was there—it was eleven o'clock at night, after all. But I thought I'd leave a message so the receptionist could get me booked first thing in the morning."

I said, "You didn't get an ambulance to take you to the hospital?"

Wilson gave me a semi-horrified look. "Of course not."

This, I reflected, was likely because of Wilson's desire to always stay somewhat in the background. That was impossible to do when arriving in an ambulance to the emergency room.

Wilson continued. "As it happened, Victor picked up the call as soon as it started ringing."

"You're kidding. He was there at eleven-thirty at night?"

Wilson nodded. "He certainly was. What's more, he told me to come right on in. Turns out, I had appendicitis. I credit Victor for allowing me to come in and helping me possibly avoid a burst appendix and life-threatening infections."

I frowned. "Please tell me that Victor just diagnosed you and then you *did* go to the hospital."

Wilson looked as if his feathers were a bit ruffled. "Yes, of course, Ann. I certainly wasn't going to balk at going to the hospital with that diagnosis. Appendicitis is nothing to mess around with. Victor drove me to the hospital himself, walked me in, and made sure I was taken back as soon as we got to the emergency room. I was incredibly impressed by him."

I had to admit, this was actually pretty impressive. That definitely seemed to be above and beyond the call of duty. Most doctors wouldn't have been at the office that late anyway, but if they *had* been and had picked up the call, they'd have told the patient to dial 911.

Wilson gave me a small smile. "So that's why I'm especially sorry to hear what happened. And sorry for you that you had to go through that this morning." He sighed again, as if feeling the weight of the world on his shoulders. "All right, well, don't let me keep you. Thanks for letting me know what happened." He paused. "As a matter of fact, what are you working on?"

I knew my answer to this was going to be key. Wilson had a habit of dumping work on me by coming up with new library events and putting me in charge of developing, scheduling, and being completely in charge of them.

"I've got the upcoming trivia night to finish planning, for one."

Wilson nodded, but I could tell that his mind was churning with new ideas for tasks for me to do. I hurriedly added, "I'm still working on the project I was researching yesterday. It's a re-source compilation for the library, designed to help job hunters find work. For it, I was pulling together books, online resources, and listing local and regional workshops that helped with re-sume-building and other skills."

Wilson nodded, looking more pleased. "Excellent. You'll make sure that the rest of the staff is aware the resource exists when you're done? I know patrons often come up to the circula-tion desk to ask questions about searching for jobs."

"Definitely. I'm also going to talk about the resource on the library's social media."

Now Wilson looked even more pleased. He didn't know much about social media except that it brought results in terms of engagement. "Anything else?" he asked.

"I also want to get started on creating a community health resource. I'll have to keep it updated, naturally, but I thought it could provide information on local support groups, fitness programs, healthcare access, substance abuse prevention and treatment, and mental health services."

Wilson looked even more cheerful now. "Very nice, Ann. That will definitely be a handy resource." He paused. "Isn't the library about to host a forum on mental health resources in the community?"

"Yes, I'm helping to set up for it. I think that's what gave me the original idea."

Wilson said the words I'd been waiting to hear: "Good job, Ann. It sounds like you've got plenty on your plate. I'll let you go get started on it all."

Chapter Four

I left his office with relief that I suddenly wasn't tasked with a local history initiative or a community survey and feedback project. As soon as I'd sat down at the desk, though, Zelda showed up and my relief was short-lived. I winced. If Zelda was approaching me at the desk, it meant she must really have something on her mind. Ordinarily, Zelda was the type of library volunteer who would snarl at patrons who approached the desk and interrupted whatever I was working on, even though I'd asked her not to.

I said, "I didn't think you were on the volunteer calendar today. You're not working at the repair shop this morning?" Zelda was a receptionist at an auto repair shop. She basically kept the place running smoothly. She'd taken the repair shop from a disorganized mess to a success with her skills in appointment scheduling, parts procurement, inventory management, and basically being some sort of administrative magician for the shop.

Zelda shrugged. "The owner is stepping in today. It's bring-your-kid-to-work day, or something. He's got his daughter there, and some mechanics are bringing their kids, too." Her face was set in grim lines. "Kids playing in the mechanics' toolboxes,

Kids taking over the customer waiting room with games of tag. Kids running everywhere. Sounded like my worst nightmare."

I was sure it did, and vice versa. I'd seen Zelda around kids at the library before, and she always seemed to scare them half to death with her austere appearance and unpredictable temper.

Zelda plunged right into what was on her mind. "I need to talk with you about the neighborhood block party. It's all a complete disaster."

It appeared Zelda was in a real state over it. She was the homeowner association president, a job she treated as if it were the presidency of the United States. The block party had been decided on by the rest of the board, and she didn't seem to be exactly overjoyed by it. Zelda was mostly a law-and-order HOA president. She was the one to drive slowly through the neighborhood, looking for tall grass, weedy driveways, and improperly stored trash bins. Fun was the last thing on her agenda. She was also the sort of person who, if tasked with doing something fun, was going to want it all to go like clockwork. Zelda's Type-A nature would allow for nothing else.

Zelda grimly continued, "Everybody in the neighborhood has got to respond to me, and they haven't been. They need to sign up for different foods and drinks. I've got this spreadsheet I made for the potluck to keep it all straight and organized. The residents need to sign up and let me know what they're bringing."

"Maybe they're not sure yet if they're going to attend," I said with a shrug.

"Another problem!" snapped Zelda. "I need to have attendance confirmation right away. Yeah, it's fine if you don't know if you're part of an event two weeks out, but this is happening almost immediately. I've emailed a bunch of people and they're not responding to me." She looked very much as if she might need one of her many daily cigarettes. Then she had a small coughing fit to indicate how much, in actuality, she needed to quit the habit.

"Okay," I said, using a steady voice to keep her calm. "What other things do you need to get confirmation about?"

"Volunteer sign-ups," she said crisply. "Set-up, clean up, emergency preparedness. All of that."

I frowned. "Emergency preparedness?"

"Of course! We're talking about a large number of people. All kinds of bad things could happen when people get excited."

I was rather doubtful that anyone would get that excited during a neighborhood block party. The event comprised kids playing, people eating potluck, and some beer consumption. But Zelda appeared to be taking the safety aspect very seriously. I guessed it wasn't a bad area to go overboard with.

Zelda continued, "It would be good if people listed on the spreadsheet whether they knew CPR. Maybe other people could monitor the kids to make sure they were safe." Zelda's expression showed that she was definitely not going to be part of the safety contingency.

"So you're trying to get a lot of information from the neighbors in a short period of time," I mused.

Zelda scowled at me. "I've been trying to get people to respond for weeks! Weeks!"

I said in a soothing tone, "I know you have. You're one of the most organized people I know. The problem is the folks in the neighborhood. Some people don't check their personal emails frequently. You could manually put paper in people's mailboxes," I said.

Zelda said, "You mean put the signups in their mailbox? But then they'd have to walk it down to me or I'd have to go around collecting them." Judging from her face, this was a completely unacceptable solution. Then she gave me a ferocious look. "Putting things in people's mailboxes is *illegal*. Those spaces are reserved for the US Postal Service."

"I'm thinking something a little different from that. Just put a colorful flyer in the newspaper slot under their mailbox. Not inside the mailbox, itself. Remind them that the full event details and the sign-up spreadsheet are in their email inbox. Tell them you need it today. Maybe having something on a physical piece of paper would be better for some people." I didn't tell her that there were plenty of younger people who barely even checked their personal email.

Zelda grumbled something I couldn't hear. "Guess I'll do that. It's a lot of work, though."

I said nothing to this because I definitely didn't want to be signed up for reminder duty.

Zelda said, "I've been working on other stuff, too. I got a city permit, so we wouldn't get in trouble for throwing an event without letting the town know."

Of course she did, although I couldn't imagine Burton would come over to break up a block party. I had the feeling that Zelda had been obsessing over this event since talk of it first started. I'd thought when she got the job at the auto repair shop and when she started volunteering at the library that she would stop obsessing over minor details like she had been. But it looked like there was still room in her day to worry over things.

"I've got extra tables for people who need them," said Zelda, ticking off items on her fingers as she spoke. "Grayson is getting the keg of beer. We're using the money from our HOA dues for the alcohol." Zelda looked distinctly irritated over this. "People need to sign up for food so everyone doesn't have cheese pizza out. I keep waking up at night having nightmares that everybody is going to pick up cheese pizza on their way home from work, and that's the only option for people to eat. We're gonna need drinks, paper products. All that stuff."

I said, "Wasn't there some discussion about not doing the potluck and just having a food truck come out to handle the food and drinks? I know there's an Asian fusion truck that's supposed to be great. And there's a taco truck that parks in the square near the library. Sometimes I'll grab a taco from there for lunch. They have a chicken Tinga taco with a smoky chipotle-tomato sauce that's to die for. Having a food truck would mean you wouldn't have to organize *anything*. It would be a lot less hassle for you and our neighbors, too. The truck would have their own plastic cutlery and napkins. They'd probably put out trash cans if we asked them. And we wouldn't have to worry about having a diverse menu. There'd be something for everybody."

Zelda glared at me, and I realized immediately that I'd said something I shouldn't. Even though she disliked the planning aspect of the block party, she clearly relished her control over the event and wasn't about to relinquish it. "Too much money!" she barked. "The HOA might need those funds for later."

I had the feeling that the homeowner's association was basically sitting on a pot of gold. Zelda was definitely the type to save for a rainy day. Who knew how much was in that account? She clearly wasn't even happy about having a keg for the block party paid from the fund.

I said in a reasonable voice, "I feel like the HOA hasn't spent any money in a long while. What types of things do you think might come up that it'll have to handle?"

"Landscaping and grounds maintenance for the entrance to the neighborhood," she muttered.

I'd noticed that it had not taken her a while to come up with that example. "Well, we always have enough in our budget for that kind of work."

"What if a hurricane comes through and blows trees down?" she asked, putting her hands on her hips.

"I guess that would be an additional expense," I agreed. "Although you know we're not prone to extreme weather here. At least, we haven't been so far."

"We're not doing a food truck," said Zelda with finality in her voice. "Now, back to the planning for the event. I also need volunteers for other things," she said, eyeing me through narrowed eyes.

I was ready for this. I'd known for a while that signing up for a tossed salad wasn't going to cut it as far as Zelda was concerned. The problem was that she saw me too often, and it was too easy for her to accost me and pressure me to help. "What do you need help for?" I asked.

Zelda started enumerating things on her fingers again. "I need help for the cleanup crew, for one."

I frowned. "Cleanup crew? I figured each homeowner would just take in the garbage from their property."

This seemed to make Zelda look rather deflated. Maybe she wanted everything to be complex and a problem to figure out. Perhaps she was deliberately making everything more complicated to make her role more important. It should be a fairly simple, fun event. "Oh. Well, I guess that's true. But I need someone to hang signs at the ends of the street saying 'no parking.' Because of the kids running around, the street will be closed off. The city seemed fine with that. Naturally, if emergency vehicles need to come through, we'll allow that."

Very generous, I thought dryly. "I'm happy to help put signs up for you, Zelda. No problem."

Now Zelda looked more cheerful. "Good. Okay, well, that's nice. Thank you." It was all said grudgingly, which made me feel as though I hadn't perhaps volunteered quite enough between the tossed salad and the signs. Then she glowered again. "There's one more thing."

I cursed myself for not escaping while I had the chance. "What's that?" I asked, summoning politeness from somewhere deep down inside me.

"The trivia," growled Zelda.

"Trivia?" It was such a quick change of subject that she lost me along the way.

"Trivia night!" said Zelda. "At the library!" She was now staring at me as if I'd lost leave of my senses.

"Oh, right. Yes, that's coming up tonight." I paused. "Were you interested in coming to it?"

I could hear the doubt in my voice. It wasn't that I thought Zelda wouldn't be good at trivia (although I couldn't imagine that she *would* be good at it). It was more that I was surprised by Zelda bringing up a library event at all. As far as I was aware, Zelda's only involvement with the Whitby library was her volunteer work shelving books.

"What are they like?" she demanded. "The trivia nights."

I considered this. "Well, we've done it a few times, although it hasn't been on the calendar lately. It's seemed pretty fun in the past. We've had a good turnout the times we've held it. The staff takes turns coming up with questions. And whoever doesn't come up with questions can join in the game, too. Wilson and I are the ones coming up with the questions this time, so I'll be the emcee. He can get fairly esoteric with the subjects he comes up with, but I think I even things out with my questions, which are more general." I frowned. "I've meant to do some promo online for trivia night, with Fitz in the photo. Maybe I can do a last-minute post."

Our social media engagement always skyrocketed whenever Fitz's furry face was part of the promo. He'd turned out to be an excellent and very patient model. It always amazed me how he seemed to realize how to sit still and pose for the camera in a very fetching manner. He'd intuitively tilt his head, arch his back, or even flash his charming feline grin. He was a natural.

"Is it full?" Zelda asked. When I didn't answer quickly enough, she said louder, "Are all the spots filled up?"

"No, I'm sure it's not full. Do you want me to register you for the trivia, just in case we get a lot of late participants signing up?"

Zelda nodded. "I'll be here."

"Hello, hello!" came a chipper voice. "How are you lovely ladies today?"

It was Luna, my colorful coworker. Luna had a fun, offbeat sense of style, which today included a flowing brown sundress covered with whimsical sunflowers. She'd paired this with knee-high socks sporting rainbow stripes. Tattoos peeked out from below the hem of the skirt and above the socks and covered her arms, and a nose-ring sat coyly on her nose. It was an outfit that wouldn't have worked for anyone else but Luna.

Zelda looked grimly at Luna, which didn't seem to faze Luna at all. Zelda grunted a greeting in response. Then she turned to me again, eyes accusing. "Why were you late today? You weren't even close to being on time. Weren't you supposed to be the one to open up the library?"

A smile tugged at my lips. Zelda was far more indignant than Wilson had been about my tardiness this morning. "I was unexpectedly held up," I said lightly. I wasn't going to give Zelda any more than that.

Zelda grunted again and said, "Better get back to it." She pushed her cart of books to shelve and trundled herself after it.

Luna waited until Zelda got out of earshot, then said, "Okay, spill it. What really made you delayed this morning? Late night with Grayson?"

I shook my head before quickly filling her in. Her eyes widened. "You're kidding. Dr. Sullivan? But he's my doctor. He was such a nice guy. What am I supposed to do now? He was the greatest."

"That's what everybody is saying. Linus told me the same thing this morning."

Luna asked, "Is Linus doing okay after finding him? That must have been awful for him."

"Luckily, he never saw Victor's body. Honestly, aside from him being upset about losing his doctor, I think Ivy had it worse. Poor dog. I could tell she felt really conflicted. Part of her wanted to pull him over to the body and part of her wanted to obey Linus. She was crying most of the time after we put her in the car. I think Linus said he would be here later today, so we'll have to check and see how he and Ivy are doing now."

Luna was barely listening. "I just can't believe anybody would murder Dr. Sullivan. That's so crazy. He was the best doctor . . . everybody loved him. He was one of those people who really made you feel *seen*. Do you know what I mean? He was so attentive whenever you were talking to him, whether it was about medical problems or stuff going on in your life. This makes me really sad."

I could tell Luna *was* really sad. What was remarkable about this is that Luna was almost always in a cheery mood. I felt the sudden need to lighten things up a bit.

"On a totally different topic, you'll never guess who's coming to trivia night tonight," I said.

"Jeremy is," she answered placidly. Jeremy was Luna's boyfriend, a boyish charmer with tousled hair and dimples punctuating his frequent grins. Although Luna was quite a bit older than Jeremy, their relationship was remarkably close. Just the mention of him made the sparkle come back into Luna's eyes.

"Besides Jeremy," I said.

Luna shook her head.

"Zelda," I said. I enjoyed seeing Luna's eyes widen again, this time in amazement.

"You're kidding me," she said. "Zelda wants to play trivia? Did you bribe her to attend? Were our attendance numbers too low or something?"

"Nope. She just wanted to come. She brought it up with me and everything."

Luna raised a pierced eyebrow. "Well, she's going to be in *such* a terrible mood when she loses. You know how good Jeremy is at trivia."

I didn't know this, but I wasn't at all surprised to hear it. Jeremy was a bright guy who seemed to be interested in a lot of different things. Plus, from what I noticed, he had a memory like a sponge. "And I guess you and Jeremy are on the same team," I said dryly.

"Of course! That's how it works. You can team up or go solo. I didn't help with creating the questions this time, so I can participate." Luna glanced across the room and said in a lower voice, "Don't look now, but there's a woman heading your way with a determined expression on her face. You're about to get pulled away."

"It could be somebody for you." I knew better, though. Ordinarily, anyone searching Luna out would have a kid or two in tow.

"See you later," said Luna, making her escape back to the children's area.

Chapter Five

The woman was definitely heading for me, but I had no problem with that. It was Veronica Carpenter, a woman in her late-forties with a sharp gaze. As usual, she was wearing dark clothing and seemed in a somber mood. She's the patron of mine who came to mind when I was listening to Dr. Lee talk about patients who might *not* have liked Victor. She and I had worked together a couple of times on research that was directly related to her dislike for Victor.

"Hi Ann," said Veronica. "Is now a good time?"

"Sure, now works great." I grabbed my laptop, and we headed off to the study area. It was a great section of the library, where any type of collaborative work could go on. It had large tables with built-in power outlets and USB ports, comfortable chairs, and great lighting. "How's everything going?" I asked, although I figured I knew the answer. It would be the same answer Veronica gave every time.

"Oh, I guess I'm getting by," she said with a shrug. Then she brightened. "I have some news to report, actually. I've decided to broaden what I'm doing with patient advocacy. I'm fortunate enough to have a little money set aside, and I'm planning to travel around to speak at medical conferences about the importance of patient advocacy and judicious testing."

"That's great!" I said, meaning it. I was glad Veronica seemed to channel the bitterness she felt against Victor into work that could benefit others. I had the feeling, looking at Veronica, that she hadn't yet heard the news about Victor. But somehow it seemed like the wrong time to interject that bit of information. Maybe because I was hoping Veronica would talk a little about her issues with the doctor. I knew that she'd had an awful experience with him, something involving her husband, but I didn't know any of the details.

Veronica smiled, looking pleased. "It was my therapist's idea, actually. She thought it was a good way to help me handle the pain I've been feeling. Since my husband died, I've felt like I've lost control over everything. His death just felt wrong, like it was never meant to happen. And my life has been off-track since then."

I nodded to encourage her, but was afraid to say anything in case Veronica stopped talking. She'd only given me the vaguest bit of information about why she was so upset with Victor Sullivan. She'd talked about negligence, and I could tell from her expression how angry she was at the doctor.

Veronica continued on, seeing I was interested. "Everybody talks about how great Dr. Sullivan is. My husband loved him, too. He always said he was such a terrific guy and that he would spend all day with you—that you never got the sense that he was rushing you out so that he could move on to the next patient."

I nodded again. "That's what I've heard, too."

Veronica said eagerly, "And that part was great. It's the first time I could actually get my husband comfortable even *going* to a doctor. He wasn't the kind of guy who wanted to darken the door of a doctor's office. If he got sick, he just wanted to hibernate in bed instead of going to the clinic. But there were things about Dr. Sullivan that weren't so great. He was a firm believer in avoiding unnecessary tests."

"Did he say why he felt that way? Or what kinds of tests qualified as unnecessary?" I asked with a frown.

Veronica wagged her finger at me. "That's exactly the point. Dr. Sullivan decided what was unnecessary and what wasn't. He told my husband that the only thing tests did was make the patient anxious and cost them money. He mentioned overdiagnosis and overtreatment. He also talked a lot about unnecessary radiation exposure."

"But your husband was experiencing symptoms that warranted having tests run?"

Veronica took a deep, shaky breath. "Sorry, I still get emotional when I talk about this." She took another breath and steadied herself a bit. "Yes, my husband was having symptoms of colon cancer. But he never discussed them with me. I guess he felt it was enough that he was talking to his doctor, a man he really trusted. Daniel probably thought that I'd only worry if he told me about his symptoms. I didn't find out about Dr. Sullivan's views on running tests until after it was clear Daniel was very sick. That's when he finally filled me in." She tightened her hands into fists. "But if he'd told me about them, he might be alive today. I'd have driven him somewhere out of town for a second opinion. Gotten an oncologist to run tests."

I said, "I'm so sorry."

Veronica was quiet for a few moments. "It was malpractice. Of course it was. By the time we finally got Daniel to another doctor, the cancer had spread everywhere, and it was too late." She swallowed a couple of times. Then she said, "You can tell this has been tough for me to get past. It all just made me so angry that I had no control over the situation whatsoever. That I couldn't do anything for my husband but watch him die. The unfairness of it all—that Dr. Sullivan was still alive and Daniel wasn't—just made me incensed."

Veronica looked over and saw my face. I wasn't sure what expressions were running across it, but I suspect she could see that I'd absorbed some of the stress that seemed to pour out of her. She gave me a small smile. "Sorry. I tend to get really intense over this stuff, which is probably why I haven't mentioned all the details to you before now. Suffice it to say, now I feel better about transferring some of my energy into doing something positive. Something that might help others."

"I'm happy to help. What are you going to focus on, in terms of research?"

Veronica looked at her notes. "I did a little digging. I'm going to need to take things broader than my own personal experience. I know we were looking at data that showed the importance of testing and catching cancers early. That's still important because I can include it in my introduction, which will be more of a personal statement." She looked again at her notes. "But I think it will be more useful, for the bulk of my speeches, to focus on interdisciplinary research. Connecting healthcare with psychology, sociology, and other fields. That way leads to a more holistic understanding of patient experience. It needs to be patient-centered instead of what works for the doctor."

It sounded to me as if Victor Sullivan *had* tried to consider patient experience holistically, however. It might have been that he simply put too much stock in a patient's test anxiety. He'd been so concerned about not putting patients through the stress and cost of testing that he'd neglected the tests altogether.

Veronica continued, "Patient advocacy goes into all sorts of areas."

"I don't know much about it. I thought it was limited to family and friends of the patient who went into an appointment with them."

"There's that, of course," said Veronica. "But there are also professional healthcare advocates, too. If I'd known about them, it really might have made a difference. They can help with navigating bills and insurance coverage, but they also can be a voice pushing for things that could help the patient. Or questioning the doctor which, in our experience, would have especially helped. We could have used someone pushing for testing, a solid treatment plan, and following-up on results and next steps."

Veronica was already eager to jump into the research and opened up her own laptop. I helped guide her to government and healthcare sites, including some research that had paywalls, since the library had subscriptions to many of the sites. We looked at medical consent forms, patient rights documents, and hospital policies for areas of improvement. We also looked at medical history and the evolution of medical practices for context on current patient care and testing standards.

Veronica said, "Okay, I think that's a good start. Maybe I'll come back over tomorrow and we can get some more data that will add depth to my talk. I also feel like the information is all over the place. I need to edit it down to make sure it's all relevant to the talks I'll give."

I said slowly, "I didn't want to hijack the whole research session, but I wanted to make sure you were aware of the news today. The news about Victor Sullivan."

Veronica's face lit up. "Did he get sued by someone else? I mean, I hate to rejoice because of someone else experiencing malpractice, but I'd love to have a partner in this fight."

I shook my head. "He died early this morning on the way to work. The police are treating it as a suspicious death."

Veronica put her hand over her mouth, her eyes wide. "No."

"I'm afraid so. I was there when he was discovered."

Veronica sat in silence for a few moments. Then she said, "This is going to be a problem for me, isn't it? I know it looks bad for me to focus on how this impacts *me*, when he's the one who's dead. But honestly? His death might bring me a little closure. It always made me so angry that he was alive when my husband was dead."

"It's going to be a problem for you?" I asked, although I knew exactly what she was getting at. She was right; she was going to be a suspect. Considering Paige Lee had brought up Veronica's anger toward Victor, Veronica was likely already a suspect, just one the police hadn't spoken with yet.

"The police are going to want to talk to me, for sure. After all, I've been speaking out against the doctor for ages. I've been very vocal. I've tried to convince people to see other physicians.

I wrote a lot online about Victor, too, which is going to be available for the police to see."

I nodded, staying quiet again.

Veronica sighed. "It wasn't that I hated the man. I honestly didn't. I didn't want anything bad to happen to him. I just wanted him to understand that he needed to change his ways. And, if he couldn't do that, which he didn't seem capable of, then I needed to let people know he wasn't a competent doctor. Yes, unnecessary testing is a bad thing. But sometimes, you have to really listen to your patient and decide to order that test, just to be on the safe side. Otherwise, you could miss something that could have dramatic consequences."

Again, it seemed to me that Victor had been nothing but a good listener. I said, "His patients always say he spends a lot of time with them in the exam room."

Veronica snorted. "Sure, he did. But half that time was spent asking patients how they were doing in their regular lives. How things were going at work or how their kids were. Small talk, basically. Yes, it made his patients love him. But it didn't help with any medical issues they might have been facing, or screening for those." She rubbed her forehead as if it was hurting. "Sorry, I didn't mean to snap at you. This news just comes as a shock. I bet the police will be in touch with me today."

I said, "Can you offer them an alibi for this morning? That should help the situation."

Veronica shook her head sadly. "With my husband gone, there's no one at home now who can verify that I was eating breakfast, drinking coffee, and getting ready for my day. Plus, I have a large property, so I don't think the neighbors can even see my driveway and verify when I left the house."

I asked, "Had you seen the doctor recently?"

"I haven't seen nor spoken with Victor Sullivan for ages. I'd decided it wasn't healthy for me to hold on to so much anger and bitterness." She gave a short laugh. "Well, my *therapist* helped me decide that. It took a while for me to come around to that way of thinking. I was working on forgiving Dr. Sullivan and making my peace with what happened. He hadn't killed my husband on purpose, after all. I don't think the doctor had a mean bone in his body. He seemed to really like Daniel, from what Daniel had told me. I've been trying to focus my energy on networking and going to this next phase of public speaking."

I said, "That seems like a great direction to go in."

"Isn't it? I feel so much better now that I have a purpose. This entire issue has given me direction. It makes me feel useful, like I'm capable of promoting change. I went to Raleigh recently and spoke to my representative there at the capitol building to share my experience. It felt good to advocate for change." She stopped short, the smile fading. "But now, it sounds like I'm going to end up being caught up in a murder investigation."

"Is there anyone you can think of who might have been upset with Victor? Maybe you can let the police know and give them another avenue to investigate," I said.

Veronica hesitated. Then she said, "Actually, there is. When I was speaking out against Dr. Sullivan on social media, I always got a reply comment from a former friend of Victor's. His name was Joel Burns. Do you know him?"

I nodded. "He spends time in the library sometimes." I didn't share that the reason he was in the library was to use our job resources. It seemed Joel was having a tough time finding work. "Do you know why he was so upset with Dr. Sullivan? Did they have a falling out?"

"I don't know. All I know is that he's been pretty angry. One time, I saw him downtown, and he came up to me to tell me I was doing a good job," said Veronica.

"A good job?"

Veronica nodded. "In my 'vendetta' against Victor Sullivan. That was the word he used. The thing was, he was obviously intoxicated. It seemed like he was really struggling . . . it looked like he wasn't taking care of himself at all. He made me worried. That's when I stopped posting stuff about Dr. Sullivan on social media."

Veronica looked behind me, and her eyes widened. She snapped her laptop closed and thrust it into her backpack. "That's Burton. I'm getting out of here. I'm not quite ready to speak with him yet."

And, in a flash, she was gone.

Chapter Six

I closed up my laptop and stood to walk over to Burton. The Library Bill of Rights requires privacy, so I wouldn't tell Burton about Veronica's issues with Victor. Luckily, Veronica had left enough of a public imprint with her allegations against the doctor that Burton wouldn't have any trouble realizing she had a strong motive. But I wanted to pass along what she'd told me about Joel Burns.

Burton smiled as I walked toward him, although his eyes held a grim expression. "I knew you had work today, but I wasn't one-hundred percent sure I'd find you here after the morning you had."

I said, "Grayson was trying to persuade me to take a personal day, but I told him the library was the best place for me."

He nodded. "I get that. Listen, I just wanted to check in with you again and see if you had any background or info for me on the doctor. I know you pick up a ton of stuff working here and talking to everybody. Hoped you had some perspective on all of this."

"I didn't really know Victor Sullivan very well, unfortunately. He wasn't my doctor. But everyone I've spoken to over the years has loved him. I've heard his praises sung for years. It was pretty shocking to me that someone had murdered him."

Burton dropped his already-low voice. "And in a way that makes it seem somebody was pretty mad at him. It felt personal. So you haven't heard of any patients who didn't like him? Not Veronica Carpenter, for instance?"

I gave him a wry smile. "I see you've already been doing some digging. You know how the library is about patron privacy. It sounds like you've probably got just as much information as I do on her." I paused. "There is something I can tell you, though. I don't know a lot about it, but I heard that Joel Burns has also been upset with Victor."

"Joel Burns?" asked Burton, taking out his notebook and making a note.

"That's right. He and Victor were once very close friends. I don't know what happened, but that apparently changed. Someone told me that Joel had even been negatively mentioning Victor on social media, so you should be able to find a trail that way."

Burton jotted down more notes. "Got it. And thanks in advance for keeping the way Victor died under your hat. I figured I didn't really need to tell you to do that."

I smiled. He'd told me without telling me. "Of course. I guessed you'd want to keep that information from getting out into the public. Grayson won't be putting it in the paper, either."

Burton nodded his head a bit absently. "There was one more thing. A jogger noticed a delivery person in the area, possibly around the time of Victor's death."

"A delivery person? That early in the morning?"

Burton said, "That's what I was thinking. I sure don't get deliveries at my house that early in the day. The jogger couldn't tell if it was a man or a woman, just saw the brown uniform. Did you see a delivery person leaving the area? Or a delivery truck?"

I took time to think back, but I knew I didn't remember any such thing. I shook my head. "The only thing I'd noticed was Linus struggling with Ivy. I'm sorry. Were there any prints or anything like that?"

"There were, but nothing in the system was a match." Burton gave me a smile. "Thanks for your help, Ann."

"Just wish I could have been more helpful. I'll keep my ears open."

After Burton left, the rest of the day went according as usual. Groups of high school students came in after school to work on projects. Adults were using nearly all the laptops in the computer room. There was a storytime for elementary kids with lots of music and laughter, courtesy of the irrepressible Luna.

I ran a couple of posts on our different social media channels, reminding library users of the upcoming trivia night. Fitz had seemed to know exactly how to pose for the promo picture, striking a very intelligent expression while surrounded with books, like someone who might be very good at trivia. At seven o'clock, I headed over to the community room where trivia night was being put on. I dragged out the popcorn machine, which was usually in use for film club and filled paper bags with popcorn. Luna had already dragged chairs out—many of them, actually, in a fairly optimistic view of how large the audience might be.

Fifteen minutes later, I was glad she'd been optimistic. We had a group of about twenty-five trivia players . . . a nice number for a town the size of Whitby.

Jeremy and Luna were sitting next to each other, and I walked over to say hi. "You're the one who came up with the questions this time?" asked Jeremy, grinning at me. "How hard are they?"

"I didn't deliberately go with 'hard.' I decided to go more with a wide range of topics. I figured that even if somebody was fantastic with entertainment trivia, they may not be on top of their game with geography."

"So you're taking the Trivial Pursuit approach," said Jeremy thoughtfully. "I approve. It's going to make things a lot tougher."

"That's why working as a team is so great," said Luna. "I can answer all the ABBA questions that Jeremy would be hopeless at. And he can give any answer that has to do with a hypotenuse."

"I'm pretty sure I didn't put a lot of math in there," I said. "Just a personal preference. But I wasn't the only person who worked on the questions. Wilson contributed a fair number, too."

Jeremy and Luna looked at each other. "I don't know if that's a good thing or a bad thing," said Jeremy slowly. He absently ran a hand through his already-tousled hair.

Luna said, "I don't even know much about Wilson's interests, except that he watches really complicated movies. What was that one that he picked for film club?"

"*2001: A Space Odyssey*," I said.

"Right," said Luna. "I mean—that movie was crazy."

"The special effects are totally amazing in it, though. Especially for the time it was created," said Jeremy.

"Sure, but I'm looking at it more from the angle that Wilson is the wildcard with the questions. Who *knows* what he might have come up with? Did you look at the questions when he sent them to you, Ann?"

I shook my head. "I ran out of time." I glanced over and saw Grayson hurrying through the door. I grinned at him. "Speaking of people who almost ran out of time, here's Grayson."

As Grayson was walking over to join us, Luna said, "I'm surprised Grayson could even find the time to be here. Victor's death is such a huge story. I bet he's going to sell tons of extra copies of the paper tomorrow."

Jeremy said, "This was what you were telling me about before we came in? About your doctor?"

"That's right. I'm still trying to wrap my head around it."

Grayson sat down next to Luna. "Hey guys. Am I part of your team, or am I going solo?"

"You're part of our team, especially if Ann told you any of the questions she was coming up with," said Jeremy with an evil grin.

"Nope, she didn't share that with me. Can I just be part of your team by my own recognizance?"

Luna pursed her lips thoughtfully. "Well, I *guess* so. Sure, enter the brain trust with us."

"Although you don't really need any help, since you've got Jeremy. He's got the memory of an elephant," said Grayson.

"Don't sell yourself short," I said. "You've got plenty to offer. Especially with your knowledge of history. Anyway, your team will need all the help it can get. I've been told a trivia expert is going to be here tonight."

Right on cue, Zelda slouched through the door. She was far out of earshot, but gave me an irritated look, just the same. I was sure she thought I should be manning either the circulation or the reference desk.

"Oh, right," said Luna in a low voice. "You said Zelda wanted to participate tonight."

"Well, good for her," said Grayson cheerfully. "Maybe we should ask her to team up."

"We can't have half the room as a team. Besides, the more people we have, the louder we have to talk amongst ourselves when we're conferring on a question. That means other people can overhear us and steal our answers," said Jeremy.

"Spoken like a true trivia expert." Luna looked admiringly at him.

Zelda didn't appear to want to join the group, anyway. She sat down fairly far away and continued scowling at the other players.

After a few minutes, during which more people trickled in, I greeted everybody, introduced myself, and kicked the game off. I got the players all warmed up with a couple of my questions: what is the capital of New Zealand, and in what country the sport of rugby originated. The next one I picked was clearly one of Wilson's. I heard everyone in the room groan when asked what ancient Greek philosopher was the teacher of Plato and the tutor of Alexander the Great. After that, there was a trick question about the smallest planet in our solar system.

I noticed about halfway through the game that Linus Truman had slipped into the room and appeared to be taking part in the game. I was both delighted and surprised to see him there. Linus was quite an introvert and also could be rather shy. He rarely attended library events, although he spent a good deal of time at the library every day. He was sitting quietly in the back, thoughtfully marking his answers on one of the answer sheets I'd put by the door. Zelda was tapping her pencil impatiently against her leg, ready to move on to the next question. She was staring at me as if I were deliberately slowing everything down.

Fitz wandered into the room, looking slightly surprised at the number of people there. I could tell he was glancing around to see who he might want to cuddle with. The cat always had an amazing ability to pick out who might be sad or hurting or having a rough day and make them feel better, at least for the short term. It was almost as if he was equipped with an innate radar. I smiled as he went unerringly to Linus. Considering Linus had the same morning I did, I thought Fitz had made a great pick.

Mona, Luna's mom and Wilson's girlfriend, was sitting next to Wilson and seemed to enjoy herself immensely by just looking around the room and listening in as people talked with others and tried to figure out their answers. Her nimble fingers worked at knitting something that looked soft and warm. The rhythmic click of her knitting needles echoed softly in the room, lending the trivia night an unexpected ambient background. Fitz watched with great interest before taking a break from Linus. In a blur of fluff and paws, he made a swift move, snagging a loose end of Mona's yarn.

He must have startled himself by his success because he leaped away, the yarn trailing like a colorful comet behind him. Mona good-naturedly disconnected Fitz from the yarn and then pulled it back toward her while Fitz executed acrobatic maneuvers in his attempts to wrest it back away from Mona. This had everyone cheering—most of them, it seemed, for the unexpectedly mischievous Fitz. When she finally recovered her yarn, Mona continued avidly listening to the game and to the different groups coming up with ideas for answers to the questions. She'd often repeat the answers out loud and Wilson would try to shush her so others wouldn't overhear them.

We progressed through questions about the author of the science fiction classic *1984* to the principal ingredient in miso soup, followed by a question about the father of modern computer science. Then time was up, and I collected all the answer sheets. The grand prize for the evening, a dinner for two donated by local restaurant Quittin' Time, was announced by Wilson to some applause. He addressed the group while I tallied up the winner.

After counting, I counted again, just to make sure. It was correct—Zelda and Linus had tied for the win and both of them had gotten nearly every answer correct. Jeremy, Luna, and Grayson had done well, too, but they scored a point behind Zelda and Linus.

Wilson finished talking, and I motioned him over. I wasn't totally sure how to distribute the prize. The restaurant had made the certificate for a party of two, and Zelda and Linus were hardly a couple. In fact, I wasn't even sure they'd ever properly been introduced to each other. Of course, both of them were at the library a good deal of the time, but there would have been no reason for the two of them to interact.

Wilson considered the problem. "I suppose the best thing to do is to announce they've won, then tell them afterward that they can either share the prize or one of them can receive a different prize. We've still got a couple of library lover's baskets left, don't we?"

I nodded. The library lover's basket was leftover from another event where we'd had prizes. It consisted of new books, a cozy blanket, and a library tote bag. It would probably work great for Linus, although I couldn't picture Zelda with the prize. However, considering she'd just tied as the winner for a trivia game, I was beginning to suspect that I didn't know much about Zelda at all.

I walked up to the microphone and simply announced the winner, as Wilson suggested. I saw Jeremy, Luna, and Grayson look slightly stunned at their loss before they all joined in the applause and genuinely cheered for the winners. Linus looked shyly pleased and Zelda rather smug, as if she'd expected no less than a win.

I thanked everyone for being there and reminded them of when the next trivia night would be held. Then I motioned for Linus and Zelda to come over. I quickly said, "I know you've both seen each other at the library, but I wanted to introduce you." I did, and Linus politely held out his hand. Zelda took it in her own unenthusiastic palm. I explained how the prize was set up and quickly offered the library lover's basket to one of them.

"I'm happy to take the basket," said Linus quickly.

Zelda thought about the options. She was giving Linus an appraising look. "Why don't we just go for the meal together? That's not a big deal, is it? I'm a library volunteer, you spend time at the library. We have that in common, anyway."

Linus's expression told me that having dinner with anybody he didn't know at Quittin' Time was the last thing he wanted to do. I suspected his idea of a perfect evening was to curl up with a nonfiction book and his dog Ivy and spend a quiet night reading, perhaps with some jazz music playing softly in the background.

But Zelda, once she had an idea in her head, was very difficult to dissuade. I had no idea why she'd focused on Linus. I doubted she had any sort of romantic attraction to him. I'd wondered before if maybe she was a little lonely. Maybe that was why she was so hyper-involved in the HOA, her job, and her volunteering. Just because she seemed prickly and unapproachable didn't mean she didn't crave socializing. As far as I was aware, outside of working, she spent her weekends quietly at home.

I wasn't at all sure how Linus was going to handle this. He was probably cursing himself for putting himself in the position to begin with. Always a gentleman, though, he politely said, "That sounds very nice. Let me know a good day and time and I'd be delighted to go to dinner with you."

Zelda gave a curt bob of her head. "Good. I'll have to check my planner." With that, she strode quickly out of the room.

I gave Linus a wry smile. "Sorry about that. I wish the restaurant had just given us two separate certificates for free meals. I'll have to ask if they can do that the next time."

"It's no bother. Perhaps I do need to go out more." He gestured around the room. "This was a fun event."

"I'm so glad you made it here," I said warmly. "And you won! I should have known you would, considering all the books and periodicals you're reading."

He looked shy again. "Oh, I've always been interested in collecting arcane bits of trivia. It passes the time." He paused. "I thought going out this evening might be good for me. Considering this morning, you know."

Linus did look tired and a bit stressed. I wasn't sure if it was from the rigor and attention resulting from the trivia game or whether it had more to do with Ivy being determined to discover a body that morning. "I'm glad you came. Your day took quite a turn pretty early this morning. Of course, I think it's easier to be around people and distracted than it is to be alone and think about what happened, which is why I came into work today, too."

"Very true, Ann."

"How was Ivy once she got home? I asked.

"She settled down nicely after I gave her some treats and a cuddle. When I left her earlier, she was napping soundly. Thanks so much for your work on the event. I'll see about coming next time." And Linus took his leave.

I walked over to join Jeremy, Luna, and Grayson again. Grayson reached out and gave my hand a squeeze. "Glad you made it," I said. "I was afraid working on the story was going to keep you from being able to come."

"It's all set," said Grayson. "The paper's ready to run the story and a profile of Victor Sullivan in tomorrow's edition. I got some help from a couple of the reporters, so it didn't take as long as it could have."

Luna said glumly, "I still can't believe it happened." She looked up at me. "Didn't I see you talking to Burton earlier?"

Luna and Burton had dated once upon a time. The relationship broke up amicably, and the two were still friends. Now they were both dating other people.

I nodded. "He came in to see if I could give any insights into what happened." I looked over at Grayson. "He mentioned a delivery person in a brown uniform being spotted by a jogger in the vicinity. Did you notice anybody like that?"

He shook his head ruefully. "I was too focused on the gym membership and then what was going on with Linus and Ivy. But it seems like a really early time for deliveries to be going on."

"I've never heard of deliveries coming prior to eight o'clock in the morning," I said. "That's what Burton thought, too. Maybe it was a cover for somebody to lurk around and wait for Dr. Sullivan to show up."

Luna shuddered. "That makes it even worse, somehow. Like some predator was just hanging around, waiting to kill him."

Jeremy put his arm around her.

I said, "I'm sure Burton and the state police will figure out who did it, soon."

Jeremy tried to inject a lighter note. "Hey, thinking back to the trivia game. Can you believe Zelda and Linus beat us?"

"Linus for sure," said Luna. "But Zelda was a total shock. Who knew she was such a scholar? And well-rounded, too. I can't believe she knew stuff about pop culture. I would never have guessed she watched new movies. I kind of had her down as somebody who would watch reruns of Newhart or Citizen Kane or something."

Jeremy nodded. "And she knew rap and hip-hop artists. I thought she'd be all about Frank Sinatra."

This launched the conversation into a much safer direction for a few minutes. Then, though, it was time for me to draw my day to a close. It wasn't my night to close up, but since I'd been so tardy to work, I stayed a little overtime to help put away the chairs and clean up the popcorn bags. Grayson gave me a hand while Luna headed back over to the children's department and Jeremy headed home.

"Was Linus doing okay after this morning? And did he give a report on Ivy?" asked Grayson.

I nodded. "He was fine. He actually seemed glad that he'd come out to play trivia tonight. And he said that Ivy had gotten lots of love and was sleeping hard when he left her."

"And you're still okay?" asked Grayson, as we walked into the library parking lot together. He carried Fitz's crate for me. "Do you want me to come home with you and Fitz for a while?"

"Honestly, I'm suddenly just dead tired. Usually, I'd love that, but tonight I think I just want to climb into my pjs and go right to sleep."

Fitz gave a dramatic yawn from his crate, one that was plainly audible. We both laughed. "Fitz is apparently in the same boat," said Grayson. "Okay, I'll check in on you tomorrow. Sweet dreams."

But I didn't end up having dreams at all. I fell deep into a dreamless sleep.

Chapter Seven

I'd slept so hard the night before that I woke up in the morning with a start. I quickly glanced at my clock and saw that I still had plenty of time before heading to the library for my Saturday shift. Fitz watched me lazily as I got up and started getting ready. Some days I fed him first, but he looked so comfy in the bed that I decided not to disturb him by pulling his food out yet.

Forty-five minutes later, Fitz and I were finally both fed and ready to head to the library. I wasn't working a full day—unless you counted the stuff I needed to do to get ready for the neighborhood block party that evening. I put a reminder on my phone to be sure and make those signs for the ends of the street that Zelda had asked me to put together. Hopefully, there would be some quiet time at work and I could get them done then.

For a Saturday morning, the library was pretty quiet. The patrons mostly comprised older adults who were catching up on reading and a few kids with their moms in the children's area. I worked for a while on medical research that someone had asked me to do for their wife's diagnosis. After I emailed the information to the patron, I worked on the library newsletter, adding in all the upcoming events. Wilson had taken photos and a bit of video of the trivia night, so I added the pictures to the newsletter and ran the video on social media.

I glanced up when the sliding doors opened and saw a young man in his mid-twenties walk into the building. He ran his hand through his carefully brushed dark hair, absently mussing it up. His hazel eyes glanced around the library before fixing on me. To my surprise, he walked up to me.

He gave me a smile. "Are you Ann?" he asked.

I smiled back at him. "Yes."

"I'm Kyle Bowman," the young man said. "Sorry to bother you. Am I interrupting you?"

I remembered Kyle Bowman was the medical student who was on a clinical rotation with Victor Sullivan and Paige Lee. "No, you're not interrupting me at all. What can I help you with?"

"I'm in here studying for an upcoming school exam, but while I was here, I wanted to ask you about Victor's death yesterday morning." Kyle paused. "You're the one who found Victor, I think. At least, that's what I heard."

Good old Whitby gossip. I nodded my head. "I'm afraid so. You're the medical student who was helping at the clinic recently?" I asked, just to show that there was plenty of gossip to go around for him, too.

"That's right," he said, looking surprised. He quickly regained his equilibrium, though. "Well, you must have had a pretty crazy morning yesterday. Were you on your way into the clinic for an appointment?"

I gave him a quick rundown of why I'd stopped by in the first place. While I was speaking with Kyle, I remembered seeing him at the library on numerous other occasions. He'd never come up to the desk before, spending his time studying, instead. On one occasion, though, I remember him asking a patron out. He definitely didn't have an issue with low self-confidence. I remembered the patron hadn't seemed to mind the attention, and she accepted his offer for a date. It took a certain amount of cockiness to pull that off.

Kyle nodded. "Got it. It's just so awful." There wasn't a lot of emotion attached to the words, though. It was almost as if he was just reciting something he knew he should say. "I'm guessing you spoke with the police yesterday, then?"

I nodded. "For a little while, yes. I'm sure they wanted to speak with you, too, considering you worked with Victor."

"They did," said Kyle with a shrug. "But I couldn't really tell them anything. I'm just knocking out the primary care portion of my medical rotation. It wasn't like I really knew Victor, or spent a lot of time with him. He was simply my supervising physician. Did the police talk to you about who they considered a suspect?"

I answered with a question of my own. "Did they tell *you* about suspects?"

I saw a flash of irritation in Kyle's eyes. "They didn't tell me anything. They were asking a bunch of questions."

"Sounds about right," I said. "They didn't disclose anything to me, either."

I couldn't tell if Kyle was relieved or worried by that. I asked, "Did they ask you if you had an alibi?"

"Sure. They said something about that being standard procedure. I was running late yesterday morning. Usually, since I'm here to make a good impression, I'm one of the first people to show up at the practice. But I've been commuting to this rotation from Charlotte, which has been driving me crazy. Driving in and out of Whitby isn't bad, but traffic anywhere close to Charlotte is out of control, even early or late in the day."

I frowned. "Commuting every day from here to Charlotte? But that's a couple of hours each way."

"This is the only rotation the school could find for me. They scouted the area, apparently. Primary care is a required rotation, so it wasn't as if I could skip it. At the beginning of our rotations, the school told my cohort they wouldn't place us farther than ninety miles away. But that just didn't work out."

"So everybody is driving these long distances?" I asked.

"I guess some of the other med students got closer assignments. The school told me it was tough to find practices willing to take students on. There's a lot of red tape involved, apparently. The clinics tell the school they have limited staff and resources, a tight schedule, or that they don't want to take on an administrative burden. Finally, I just couldn't take the drive anymore. I started looking around here for a place to stay that was reasonable. I just found a local place day-before-yesterday . . . an Airbnb to rent until I finish the rotation."

I nodded. "That makes the most sense. I'd be nodding off in the car if I had to make that drive after a long day working."

"Yeah, it makes the most sense, but it's definitely the more expensive option, although gas for the commute wasn't cheap, either. The commute was just way too long, even though I was passing the time listening to medical podcasts. Anyway, yesterday morning at the rental, nothing was working. It's a cheap place to stay, obviously, but you kind of have expectations that stuff's going to work, right? My alarm didn't go off, or else I slept through it. The microwave wasn't working, so I couldn't heat my frozen breakfast biscuits I'd gotten from the store. I knew I was going to have to get something to eat before I went in to work, but it couldn't be something hot. I ran by the store to pick up cereal and milk. On the way, though, I saw all the emergency vehicles."

"You didn't stop?" I asked.

Kyle shook his head. "Nope. I figured one of the patients who was waiting for us to open had an episode or something. I went home, ate real quick, and was about to head out to the clinic when Dr. Lee called and told me we weren't going to see any patients yesterday."

"And you're obviously not working today," I said.

He shook his head. "I just need four shifts a week for school. I already worked them for the week, so having yesterday off and today isn't a problem. I needed time to study this afternoon, anyway, and probably relax a little. That commuting was getting to me."

"Is Dr. Sullivan's death going to affect your rotation in a big way?"

Kyle frowned. "Yeah, probably. I was thinking about that yesterday. He was my supervising physician. When Dr. Lee called me to give me the news, she told me she was calling my school and letting them know that she'd be taking over as my supervisor." He paused. "I was just glad she was willing to take on the responsibility. Otherwise, I'd be up the creek without having my primary care rotation finished. Like I said, the school was having a tough time placing all the students into rotations. In some ways, working with Dr. Lee will probably be easier. But of course, it will be an adjustment."

"Did you and Dr. Sullivan get along well?"

Kyle said, "We got along fine. There was never any trouble between us or anything. I mean, primary care hasn't been my favorite rotation so far, but it's okay. I'm getting my hours in, and, like I was saying earlier, it's required, so it's not like I could get out of it. The good thing has been that, in a small town like Whitby, I'm getting the opportunity to do a lot more things. Patients come into the practice for all sorts of stuff that they might see specialists for in a bigger town. I've been able to do dermatology procedures and things like that."

"And Dr. Sullivan was easy to work with?" From what Dr. Lee had said, Victor Sullivan was anything but easy to work with, in terms of the staff. I was curious to see if Kyle was going to spin it.

"The only thing I didn't really like about Victor was the way he worked with his patients," said Kyle.

"He didn't have a good bedside manner?"

Kyle snorted. "He'd spend all day with one patient! The man couldn't stay on schedule to save his life. I'd be trying to work through as many patients as I could, as quickly as possible, and we were still running behind. If that happened in Charlotte, the patients would riot in the waiting room. It made me so frustrated. It felt like Victor didn't have any respect for his patients' time. Plus, he was really into the homeopathic stuff."

"He didn't prescribe a lot of medication?"

Kyle said, "I'm not saying he didn't dole out blood pressure meds or other maintenance drugs. But if he had the chance, he'd avoid an antibiotic for a homeopathic option. I mean, that's fine. That's his choice. But he didn't seem to trust many of the new medicines. And he wasn't familiar with some of the drugs I knew about. I don't think he kept up with ongoing education. As far as I'm aware, Victor didn't attend conferences or read medical journals or that kind of thing."

Dr. Lee had thought Victor read journals, though, even if he could be mistrustful of, or reluctant to try new procedures and drugs. And he'd had a large medical reference book next to him when I found him.

"I guess he was too busy keeping up with the patients," I said. "Was it usually busy in the clinic?"

Kyle said, "It was always hopping. Packed. We always had tons of people in the waiting room."

"It's hard to believe someone did this to him. Did you come across any patients or staff who seemed to have a grudge against him?"

Kyle said, "I was thinking about that last night. If the police have a lead, the heat will be off me. I don't need anything to jeopardize this rotation of mine or my medical career. While I was thinking it through last night, I remembered Dr. Lee and Dr. Sullivan never seemed to get along well."

I thought again about how cold Paige Lee had seemed when she was talking about her coworker. "The two of them argued in the office?"

"Nothing like that," said Kyle. "They were both very professional. But there was just a lot of tension and bad feelings there. I caught Dr. Lee staring at Victor's back once, and her eyes were just full of hatred."

"Really?" asked Ann. "That's a strong word."

"There's not a better word for it. Not just the irritation that you might have with a roommate or something. Full-fledged hatred. One nurse told me Victor and Paige had once been an item. I totally can't picture that. If it was true, and the nurse insisted that it was, then Paige must have been the one to dump Victor. Because she sure seemed furious and fed-up with him."

It was interesting that Dr. Lee and Kyle were blaming the other for having a tough relationship with Victor.

I said, "Probably working in a small clinic with him didn't help with the tension."

Kyle shrugged. "That's why you're not supposed to have relationships with people you work with. Everybody knows that. You've got to date somebody outside the office instead."

"Was there anybody else besides Dr. Lee who seemed upset with Victor?" I asked.

"Yeah, there was that patient who's made all the fuss. In a town this size, you've got to know who I'm talking about. She's always talking about Victor on social media and probably tells everybody she comes across about her issues with him. I'm surprised she wasn't staging protests in the street in front of the clinic."

I nodded, since Kyle seemed to wait for an answer. Veronica Carpenter, who'd I'd been helping yesterday with her patient advocacy research.

"That woman was full-on furious with him. She kept showing up unexpectedly at the clinic and giving Victor a piece of her mind, usually in front of other patients. I don't know the entire story, since it was before my rotation started, but she definitely isn't the type to let anything go. I got that she was mad Victor didn't run tests as a response to her husband's symptoms. Believe me, I wouldn't have done the same thing in Victor's shoes."

I remembered what Dr. Lee had said about Kyle wanting to embrace medical innovations and technology. "You'd have run the tests, based on what her husband was telling Victor?"

"Oh yeah, without a doubt. Victor acted like he lived in the past. Almost as if he was reluctant to use all the modern tools we have now. What's the point of living in the twenty-first century if you practice medicine like it's 1970?"

I said, "So you think the woman's anger was justified?"

Kyle said, "I'd have been mad too, if it was somebody I cared about. Although she's taking things way too far now. I've read some things she's posted on social media—I looked up her posts when one nurse was telling me about it. At this point, it's almost like she's trying to find a scapegoat for her husband's death. Like she's having a tough time processing his death and moving forward. She wanted to blame a *person* instead of the cancer. But the cancer is the whole reason he's gone."

Kyle paused for a second, giving me a measuring look. "Anyway, that's all I know about that. Hopefully, the cops will find somebody who's a better suspect than I am. On a totally different topic, is there anything fun to do around this town? Now that I'm not commuting from Charlotte, I thought I'd try to check things out here in Whitby. I'll have extra time on my hands without the driving."

The way he was looking at me and the lightness of his tone made it hard for me to tell if he was being flirtatious or whether he was genuinely interested in hearing about Whitby's attractions. In the off-chance that he was actually wanting to know, I stepped back into librarian mode. "It's a great place to be if you're interested in outdoor activities. There are some nice hikes to take, with amazing views. There are a few cool waterfalls that you can picnic or camp out near. I always find that really relaxing. We have the lake, too, and you can rent kayaks or go fishing."

Kyle gave me a smile. "Would you be interested in going with me? On a hike, I mean? Or dinner, maybe?"

I smiled back. It seemed a little like half-hearted hitting on me. I didn't get the impression he was at all serious about it or really even very interested. "Thanks for asking, but I'm in a relationship right now."

Kyle sighed. "Like everyone else in this town. It's a rotten place to meet anybody. Okay, well, if anything changes with your relationship status, just let me know." He gave me a cocky smile and headed off to the study area with his backpack.

Chapter Eight

I got a good deal of stuff done after Kyle headed out. I needed to create promo for some of the upcoming library events, so I recruited Fitz into the effort. Although he'd been sleeping happily in a sunbeam, he got right into modeling mode, giving me a bunch of fetching feline smiles. I ended up with a bunch of material that I could use for the month.

I laughed out loud making one of them. I'd used some design magic to make Fitz look as if he was a book critic. I used Photoshop to outfit him in reading glasses, a bowtie, and a tweed jacket. He was staring thoughtfully at the camera and surrounded by books. Then I worked on another one to promote our mystery collection, with Fitz in a Sherlock-esque deerstalker hat and holding a magnifying glass in front of his face.

After a while, Linus walked up to the reference desk. He'd been sitting, in his suit, of course, in the periodicals section, completing his usual morning routine of nonfiction, fiction, and magazine reading. I smiled at him. "How's our big trivia winner?"

"Fine," he said with a small smile of his own. "Although I had a tough time falling asleep last night. I guess it must have been all the excitement of the game. I ended up making myself a glass of warm milk, and that helped."

"Did it?" I asked in surprise. "I'd somehow always thought that was an old wives' tale."

"Apparently, it has something to do with melatonin and tryptophan," said Linus with a small shrug. "The milk settled me down a little. I'm not used to being out that late."

It hadn't been late, of course, but I suspected that Linus probably rarely left his house again after returning from the library about four in the afternoon.

Linus said, "Zelda called me up after I got home and set up the dinner for tomorrow night." He gave me a pained smile. "It'll be fine."

I felt bad for him. I couldn't imagine spending an hour or more in Zelda's cranky company. "Sorry about that. I'll fix it so prizes don't work that way in case of any future ties at library events."

Linus looked a bit worried. "You don't think Zelda considers this a date at all, do you? I think that may have been part of the reason I was up last night. I was wondering if I needed to purchase her a corsage or chocolates or something."

"Do you *want* it to be considered a date?" I asked in a doubtful voice.

He shook his head. "No, not at all. Nothing against Zelda, of course. I'm afraid that, after losing my wife, I'm simply not interested in seeing anyone else."

I knew Linus hadn't recently lost his wife . . . that it had been some time ago. But he and his wife had obviously been soulmates, and he seemed like a one-woman guy. I said, "I didn't get the slightest impression that Zelda considered this to be a date. She's a fairly pragmatic woman. I think she didn't want to waste the extra meal she'd won." Pragmatic was one way of putting Zelda. There were other less complimentary adjectives, but I didn't want to make Linus more concerned about his dinner than he already was.

Linus looked relieved. "Okay, good. Thanks, Ann. That makes me feel a lot better." He hesitated. "I believe I spotted you speaking with Kyle Bowman."

"That's right. Do you know him?"

Linus said, "Not really. I have seen him from time to time in the clinic when I couldn't get in to see Victor Sullivan."

"What do you make of him?"

"He was very professional. I'm sure any issues I might have had were because of me, not him. But Kyle was in such a rush. I could tell he was a very bright young man, but I wasn't used to being hurried out of the exam room. Maybe I got spoiled by my years of seeing Victor. Kyle wanted to push things along the whole time. Unfortunately, I'm an old man and some things just can't be hurried. Kyle cut me off a few times when I was trying to describe different symptoms I was experiencing." Linus sighed. "It was all rather frustrating."

"I'm sure it was. Do you have any upcoming appointments?" If he did, it was going to make him even more frustrated than he already was. The clinic was going to be teeming with patients, with Victor gone.

"Fortunately not," said Linus somewhat fervently. "I can only imagine how busy it will be over there with Victor gone and Dr. Lee and Kyle taking over his patients. Plus, I'm just not sure if I'll be able to warm up to Dr. Lee. She also seems very knowledgeable and professional. But there's no genuine kindness there, is there? Not like there was with Victor."

I grabbed a piece of paper and wrote my doctor's name. Then I looked up the phone number and address and added them down on the paper, too. "In case you want to change to another clinic, here's my doctor's information. I really like her. I'm not sure she takes *quite* as much time as Victor did, but she never seems in a rush. She also has a really warm, caring manner. But if you're going to change doctors, I'd go ahead and call as soon as possible before word gets out and everyone thinks about making a switch."

Linus chuckled. "I'm sure word has already gotten out. I read Grayson's excellent article in the paper this morning, along with his equally well-written profile of the good doctor."

"True," I said with a rueful smile. "Then time really is of the essence."

"I'll make a new patient appointment with your doctor as soon as I get home today," promised Linus with a smile before he disappeared back into the periodical section.

The rest of my shift at the library was a fairly quiet one. I had no trouble getting out in time to get set up for the block party in my neighborhood. Fortunately, I'd remembered to make the signs at work and also remembered to bring them back home with me. I put together the salad I was bringing as my food contribution, although I wasn't certain salad might be particularly in demand during a block party that featured a keg. The nice thing was that it was inexpensive and easy to make. I threw in cherry tomatoes, sliced radishes, shredded carrot, and some feta cheese.

I hung the colorful signs up on the ends of the street right before the designated time, then set up my table in my driveway. I placed the salad there, carefully covered with plastic wrap, along with paper plates and forks. Grayson came right up to see me, giving me a hug. "Hey there! I wanted to come by and eat your salad first thing."

I gave him a wry smile. "Because you've been just dying for a salad all day? That's sweet of you. I had the feeling I might not get much business over here today."

We glanced up and down the street. It looked like everybody had taken part. I'd wondered if there might be a couple of holdouts, especially since Zelda had been worried about people responding. Some people had colorful balloons on their mailboxes. Tables were lined up along the sidewalk with food and drinks and seemed to hold an array of homemade dishes. Zelda must have gotten the signups to work as she'd wanted because there was no sign that everyone had picked up cheese pizza. Neighborhood kids were taking advantage of the blocked-off street by playing tag and hide-and-seek. Someone had brought a boombox outside, and it was playing festive music.

"It looks like the party's a success," said Grayson cheerfully. "Zelda's going to be really pleased."

"Zelda's going to be nothing of the sort," I said with a snort. "She'll be sure to find a problem with the block party, no matter what. You know what a perfectionist she is."

"True," said Grayson. "Well, I got the keg set up, which was my appointed task."

"No food table for you?" I asked curiously.

"I decided at the last minute to pick up a cheese pizza on my way back from getting the keg and set it up in my yard. Figured that might take care of some of the kids who're here."

Our neighborhood didn't have a lot of kids in it, but I was sure the ones we did have would prefer pizza to salad. "Good thinking," I said. I hid a smile. Hopefully, Zelda wouldn't go off on Grayson for randomly picking up the dreaded cheese pizza without signing up for it on her spreadsheet.

Grayson said lightly, "Hey, I also wanted to see how you were doing after yesterday. That was a crazy-long day for you. We were up before dawn heading to the gym, then you had a full day at the library after finding Victor. You seemed pretty good at trivia night. Were you able to get any sleep last night?"

"Yeah, I slept like the dead, actually." Then I winced. "Poor choice of words."

"Glad you could get some shut-eye. Sometimes when I have a busy day, it's almost like my brain doesn't want to turn off."

I said, "That's usually my problem, too. I guess I must have been exhausted enough to override that issue. By the way, I wanted to let you know you had a great article this morning. Actually, great *articles*. The story covering Victor's death was good, and the profile of him was especially nice. Linus mentioned the same thing when I spoke to him earlier."

Grayson looked pleased. "Did you think so? I've always got some latent insecurity about running those profiles. I have to make them sound insightful and authoritative, like I know what I'm talking about. It isn't easy when I'm still a newcomer in town. Plus, of course, I didn't know Victor at all."

"Well, the quotes you got from people really helped fill in any gaps there might have been. It was a great piece."

Grayson said, "Off-the-record, of course, but did you hear anything helpful while you've been out and about? Get any insights on Victor, or who in town might be considered a suspect?"

I said, "A little, I guess. Of course, I already told you about Paige Lee yesterday."

"Right. Victor's colleague at the clinic. It sounded like she wasn't too broken up when she heard about Victor's death."

I nodded. "Or maybe she just keeps a tight leash on her emotions; it's hard to say. She definitely disapproved of Victor's patient-centered approach to appointments and how far the clinic ran behind schedule. I found out today from Kyle Bowman that she and Victor had been in a relationship at one time. At least, that's what Kyle heard from the staff at the clinic."

Grayson raised his eyebrows. "You're kidding."

"I know. I was shocked, too. It sounded like they had nothing at all in common."

Grayson said, "I guess opposites can attract."

I grinned at him. "They did in our case, anyway."

"Are we really opposites? I'm not so sure."

I said, "Think about how extroverted you are compared to me. You're always more interested in going out at night and seeing people. Or going to cookouts and tailgates. I'm the one who wants to curl up on my sofa with a book and my cat."

"That's true," said Grayson. "Although you rally to the occasion really nicely when we do go out. You also spend most of your day with people at the library, so it's not like you're not around people."

"Right, but that's kind of in a different capacity, isn't it? I'm rarely just overtly socializing there, unless I'm talking with Luna. It's more like I'm helping people out. Maybe that's what makes it easier. Anyway, yes, that's what I heard about Dr. Lee and Dr. Sullivan. They'd dated before. Keep in mind, like I mentioned, that I found that out third-hand. It's sort of like the game of telephone—you're never sure if what you're hearing is entirely accurate."

"Kyle Bowman," said Grayson with a frown. "I'm trying to remember who he is."

"He's the medical student who came into the library this morning. He'd heard I'd found Victor and wanted to pump me for information. He was less interested when he realized I knew about as much about Victor's death as he did," I said. "Paige Lee had said Kyle and Victor didn't work together really well."

"Were you able to ask Kyle if that was true?" asked Grayson.

"He talked a little about his work relationship with Victor. Victor served as his supervising physician for the rotation. Kyle didn't have any alibi for yesterday morning because he was out running errands. He'd been commuting from Charlotte every day and just settled into some sort of rental where nothing works."

Grayson gave a low whistle. "Commuting from Charlotte? That's quite a drive."

"He was driving four hours a day. It sounded like he was trying to save money instead of getting a hotel room or renting an

Airbnb. Anyway, he also complained about Victor spending so much time with each patient."

"Yeah, that would be annoying. I'm guessing Dr. Lee and Kyle were having to pick up the slack when the waiting room was full. But is that really a motive to kill somebody? It sounded like this was a planned murder, right?"

"Maybe," I said. "The killer used improvised weapons. The murder weapons were Victor's own stethoscope and book. But it seems to me like the murderer must have been lurking around, waiting for the doctor to show up for work." I hesitated. "There's someone else who makes for a good suspect. I can't give much information because it's one of my patrons. This person was unhappy about what they considered malpractice by Victor."

Grayson nodded. "When I was working on my profile piece yesterday afternoon, I came across Veronica Carpenter while researching online for information about Victor. I'm guessing that's who you're talking about. She had a real vendetta against him online, posting all the time."

"Kyle mentioned she showed up at the clinic sometimes, too," I said. "He said she would tell Victor off in front of his own patients sometimes."

"Nice," said Grayson.

I said, "I'd forgotten that Victor was divorced until I read your article this morning. You didn't get a quote from his ex-wife, I noticed."

Grayson snorted. "Not a chance. I called and asked if she wanted to contribute a brief statement about Victor for the profile I was working on. She couldn't get off the phone fast enough."

"Too bad," I said. I thought for a moment. "I'm guessing an ex-wife would be on Burton's list of possible suspects."

Grayson shook his head. "It doesn't sound like she'll be on his list at all. I'd gotten her phone number from a friend of a friend of a contact. She was on the other side of the country, sightseeing."

"She'd heard the news about Victor, though?" It made me anxious to think of calling somebody up and having to tell them about somebody's death, even if it had been an ex.

"Fortunately, yes. And perhaps not surprisingly, considering how Whitby is. I'm sure somebody called or texted her as soon as the news was out. Or maybe the police reached out."

"I wonder if Victor was dating again."

Grayson smiled at me. "You must have been pretty distracted while you read that profile piece."

I chuckled. "I probably couldn't pass a reading comprehension test that early in the morning. Why?"

"Victor remarried last year. He married the woman he was having the affair with. And his wife's ex-husband is coming down the street toward us right now."

Chapter Nine

Ilooked to see a man in his early 50s with untamed gray hair heading our way. He was rugged looking, as if he'd worked with his hands or possibly his back every day for years. He was grasping a plastic cup that I guessed might hold a bit of the keg in it.

"How's it going?" he asked us. He smiled at me. "I don't think I know you. I'm Roger Driscoll."

"Ann Beckett," I said, reaching out to shake his calloused hand. "Good to meet you."

"Any friend of Grayson's is a friend of mine," he said. He looked at our empty hands. "Am I the only one taking advantage of the keg? I thought that's what the thing was for."

"We just haven't made it over there yet," I said with a smile. Although I wasn't planning on drinking beer at all. I thought I might grab a plastic cup and pour some wine from my fridge into it. Although that might provoke the wrath of Zelda, who was likely to fret again about the cost of the beer keg if there were lots of leftovers.

"Well, you better get over there soon or else I'm going to look at it as my duty to drink the keg dry," he said, grinning. "Waste not, want not."

"I don't think I've seen you around the neighborhood. Are you new here?" I asked. "Or is this a sign that I've been working too much and haven't taken enough walks in order to meet you?"

"You've been working too much," said Grayson, a twinkle in his eye.

Roger said, "You're working too much, but I'm also new here. Grayson and I met up when he was taking a jog a week ago or so." He pointed down the street. "I bought that little brick house."

It was a one-bedroom from the 1930s, if I remembered right from the last time I'd been in there. "Great location," I said. "I really like this neighborhood because it's so central to everything. Plus, the neighbors are great." Besides Zelda, although that was a topic for another time.

Roger took a huge slug from his cup. Now that I was looking more closely at him, it looked as if maybe he'd enjoyed pre-party beverages before the block party started. He swayed slightly on his feet as if he wasn't drinking his first beer of the night. "Yeah, everybody has been great so far. But I wasn't planning on living here, you know. I had a much bigger house before this one. It was sort of an unexpected downsize."

Grayson cleared his throat. "Roger actually helped me out yesterday with the profile I wrote on Victor."

Roger squinted at him through bloodshot eyes. "You didn't use much of it, though." He frowned. "Don't think you used *any* of it."

Grayson said in a cheery voice, "But everything you gave me was great background. I need information in order to provide context for what I was writing."

I must have looked as curious as I felt because Roger leaned closer. "I'll tell you all about it. Let's just say I'm not sorry Victor is gone."

I figured this probably had something to do with the fact that Victor had been married to Roger's ex-wife, but I didn't want to divulge that I already knew this. "You were a patient of his?"

Roger snorted. "I was a *neighbor* of his. Before the guy took everything I had in life. My wife, my house."

"He took your *house* away from you?" I stared at him.

"Not like that," said Roger, waving an unsteady hand. "But just about as bad. The house had been in my family for a long time. My folks were successful people here, and so were my grandparents. Big house with a verandah curving around the front. It had all kinds of curlicues—like this real elaborate gingerbread trim. And pointed gables on top. My parents passed away some time ago, and I ended up with the house. Of course, I loved the place. I'd grown up there when my grandparents gave the house to my parents."

"How did you end up losing it?" I asked, frowning.

"Well, it was personal preference, I guess, although I was pushed into it. You see, my wife and I lived right next door to Victor. Of course, I got the house in the divorce, but I couldn't stand to have Cheryl and Victor living next door to me. So I moved over here." He gave a short laugh. "The cops were talking to me earlier today. Guess they figured I killed Victor. I must have shot my mouth off too much, telling everybody my story, just like I'm doing now. I can't help being bitter about it. I never had a clue Cheryl and Victor were seeing each other on weekends while I was out of the house working."

Grayson said in a sympathetic voice, "I'm really sorry to hear that. You must have hated selling your family home."

"You bet I did. But what else was I going to do? My house had a full view of their back deck. I kept seeing the two of them cozying up on their deck, drinking wine, toasting each other. It was driving me crazy. But *not* crazy enough to kill the guy."

"Did you give the cops an alibi? I bet that got them off your back," said Grayson.

Roger glowered. "Nope. Don't have an alibi. I'd have had an alibi if I still had my wife living with me. Of course, Victor took care of that. But I haven't been over to that house since the divorce, so I'd never have been able to walk over and kill Victor. Makes me sick to even look at the house. I take the long way to work, when I *am* working, just so I don't have to drive by it."

I noticed Roger seemed to think Victor had been murdered at home, instead of at his office.

"What kind of work do you do?" I asked.

Roger took another big sip of beer as if he desperately needed the fortification. "Construction. I do a little bit of everything. Carpentry, masonry, general labor. Whatever they need me to do." He straightened, suddenly looking defensive. "I work hard and do a good job. Show up on time, don't take a lot of breaks. I'm a good employee."

Grayson said, "And good, skilled employees are worth their weight in gold these days." He paused. "I guess you probably haven't spoken to Cheryl, your ex-wife, since Victor died."

Roger snorted again. "Oh, I've spoken to her, all right. She was the one who called me up after Victor died. Cheryl was totally hysterical, blaming me for killing him. I told her I had nothing to do with it. I'd been nowhere near that house, like I said."

This was the second time Roger made an allusion to staying away from "the house," as if he thought Victor died there. Grayson seemed to notice the same thing. But wouldn't the police have asked if he'd been near the clinic, where Victor actually died?

Grayson said, "I suppose Cheryl is probably a suspect herself, isn't she? Usually the spouse is so often at fault in murder cases."

"Not this time," said Roger. "She was at the beach with her girlfriends when the cops called to tell her. Now she can do fancy vacations, since she was married to Victor." He brooded on that for a few seconds before having another gulp of beer.

"What was your relationship with her like?" I asked. Grayson gave me an appreciative look for asking the question. I knew that if Grayson asked too many questions that Roger would back off, thinking he was being interviewed for the paper.

A wistful expression crossed Roger's face. "I thought we had ourselves a great relationship. It felt like we were a good match—like we were meant to be. I always felt like I was sort of living in a fairytale with Cheryl. We started out as high school sweethearts. Not too many people end up marrying their high school girlfriends, you know. I was a football player, not a real good one, and she was a cheerleader. She was an awesome cheerleader. She was one of those fliers, you know. The kind that the other girls throw up in the air to do tricks and stuff." He looked lost in his memories.

"You got married right after school?" I asked.

"That's right. Well, after Cheryl got done with college. She was good with business, you know. She was a CPA. Had her head right on her shoulders, at least for a while." His mouth twisted in a bitter smile. "We did all kinds of outdoorsy, cheap stuff together. Hiking, camping, picnics. I had a canoe, and we'd go out on the lake together, share a bottle of wine and watch the sunset." He laughed. "Cheryl even enjoyed fishing, so we'd try to fish off the canoe without tipping the thing over. We'd buy some bait at the bait shop and set out. I can't even imagine what she and Victor had in common. I don't think that guy spent a lot of time outdoors." He shrugged, tearing up a little. "I guess she suddenly got more interested in money and her lifestyle. She was done with our cheap dates."

"Do you have any idea who might have done this to Victor?" asked Grayson. "It seems to me that the cops won't pressure you as much if there's someone else who seems like a better suspect."

Roger relaxed at this idea. Or maybe it was the beer kicking in. "Well, that's a good point, Grayson. I'll have to think about that. All I hear about is everybody singing Victor's praises. It's tough to find somebody with a different point of view. Besides, I didn't even really know the doctor, except as a neighbor."

"What was he like as a neighbor?" I asked.

"You mean before he started messing around with my wife? I always got the feeling Victor was looking down on me somehow. Like I wasn't good enough to be his neighbor. I mean, Cheryl and I had a nice house. A lot nicer than the house I'm living in now. But it wasn't anything like that mansion he lives in."

I said, "I'm surprised to hear Victor was condescending to you. I'd have thought he'd want to be on good terms with his neighbors."

"He was on good terms with my wife, that's for sure," said Roger. He took a last gulp of his beer, then looked sadly into his empty cup. "Yeah, I don't know. Maybe part of it was me having a chip on my shoulder because I work a blue-collar job, and he was a doctor. But I kind of doubt it. I've never been ashamed of my job. Construction is something I've always enjoyed, and it's what I'm good at. No, I think it was really just Victor thinking I was a smaller person than he was."

He paused, then wagged his finger at us. "The thing is, Victor got a better start in life than I did. He didn't even have to buy that big house he had—that had been in his family for generations. I bet he didn't even have to pay loans for med school."

Grayson seemed to try to get the conversation back on track. "So you can't think of anybody who was upset with Victor, then?"

After a moment, Roger wagged his finger at us again. "There is one guy I can think of. He's got just as much reason to be upset with Victor as I had. Joel Burns. He used to be good buddies with the doctor."

I remembered Veronica telling me about Joel Burns and how he'd chimed in on her social media posts, agreeing with her about how awful Victor was. I wondered again what Joel's reason was for going from good friend to enemy in what sounded like a short amount of time.

Roger continued. "Joel and I hung out together sometimes, too. Haven't seen him for a while, though. Know why I haven't seen him? That's because of Victor and how he messed up Joel's life."

Grayson leaned in a little. "Really?" he asked. "I haven't heard about that."

Roger said slowly, "It really isn't my story to tell, but basically, Victor broke up Joel's marriage."

I said, "Victor had an affair with Joel's wife?"

"No, not that time. That just happened with *my* wife," said Roger sourly. "But he just as effectively broke it up." He stumbled a little over the word *effectively*.

"How did he do that?" asked Grayson.

Roger paused. "You know, I think I've been running my mouth too much. I'm going to grab a refill and maybe get something to eat." He glanced down at my salad, not apparently considering it to fall under the edible category. "Good talking to you two. Thanks for the welcome to the neighborhood."

Roger wandered away, not entirely in a straight line. I saw Zelda, who seemed to have put herself on supervisory duty, narrow her eyes at him. This might be the last time a keg made its appearance at one of our block parties.

Chapter Ten

G rayson said, "Well, that was a lot to unpack. I feel sorry for the guy, though. I think the loss of his wife really hit him hard."

"His house, too," I said. "But I totally understand where he was coming from. Of course he wouldn't want to live next door to his ex-wife and her new husband. Why would he? It makes sense that he'd move away and buy something over here." I paused. "Did you notice he seemed to think that Victor was murdered in the house?"

Grayson nodded. "I wonder if he was just trying to show that he didn't know anything about the murder. Or if he genuinely *didn't* know anything about it."

"Or if he was just too intoxicated to remember what the cops had told him," I said dryly. "All of those things are possible."

Grayson asked, "Do you know this Joel Burns he was talking about?"

"Some. I've seen him at the library before." I frowned. "Wait a minute. I think I've seen his name recently somewhere else." I pulled out my phone.

"On social media, maybe?"

I shook my head. "I haven't really been online that much lately, aside from doing research." I scrolled through my Google docs on my phone. "Here it is. He's one of the speakers on the mental health and well-being panel we're hosting at the library on Monday."

"Oh, right, I remember seeing that and thinking I needed to send one of our reporters to cover the panel. But if Joel is going to be a speaker, I'd like to be there myself." Grayson took out his own phone. "I'll make sure the panel is on my calendar for Monday."

A scratchy voice said, "You guys shouldn't be on your cell phones during the block party."

We turned like guilty children to find Zelda glowering at us. I put away my phone hastily. "I was just checking on a library event, Zelda."

This didn't appease her, however. "You're off work. You should be having *fun*."

Grayson and I hastily assured her we *were* having fun, although possibly not right at that second. We put our phones in our pockets.

"Things are going great with the block party, Zelda," said Grayson, giving the woman a reassuring grin.

Zelda, however, looked pretty strung out and as if she might pull out a cigarette at any time. I had the feeling she didn't care much about being a hostess. She *wasn't* a hostess, of course, but she seemed determined to fill that role.

Zelda croaked, "Not really. People aren't following my guidelines."

There was no way to argue this. No matter what people were doing, Zelda would think they were breaking the rules.

Now Zelda turned her focus completely on me. I wondered what sort of infraction I'd committed. I saw Fitz watching us from the cottage window, his tail wrapped around his feet. Zelda said, "Saw you talking to that murderer yesterday."

I blinked at her. "I'm pretty sure I didn't speak with any killers. Where? At the library?"

Zelda made a scoffing sound as if to say I didn't go anywhere else *but* the library. She wasn't all that wrong, of course. "You were talking to that Veronica Carpenter."

So much for patron privacy. Zelda just guaranteed that Grayson knew for sure the identity of the patient who was so unhappy with Victor.

Before I could say anything in Veronica's defense, Zelda continued in a furious tone. "Dr. Sullivan was *my* doctor. I know that woman is responsible for his death. She killed *my doctor*."

Zelda clearly viewed Victor Sullivan's death as a personal affront. She added, "The woman who's always taking you away from your work."

I stifled a sigh. Zelda couldn't seem to get it through her head that a big part of my job as a reference librarian was to sit down with patrons and assist them with projects. I tried again, as Grayson gave me a sympathetic look. "Research is an important aspect of my work."

"I'm not having that," snapped Zelda. Now she did take out a cigarette. "I know that woman did it. I saw her. Yelling at him. Now I have to go find another doctor."

Grayson asked, "You saw this Veronica yelling at Victor? When was that?"

Zelda gave Grayson a grim smile, as if rewarding him for fully comprehending the issue. "Thursday. It happened Thursday."

That was the day before Victor's murder. I said, "You actually *saw* this? Veronica told me she hadn't spoken to Victor Sullivan in a long time."

"Of *course* I saw it! Right in the street outside the grocery store. She *yelled* at him. And Dr. Sullivan just looked like he wanted to get away from her. But she didn't have to kill him. I don't like having to find a new doctor."

Grayson said, "No, that's really difficult. I'm sorry, Zelda."

Zelda rewarded him with another smile. Then her expression darkened again. "Saw you talking to Roger. That guy is causing me a headache," she said, glaring at Roger's back. I was thinking Roger had perhaps escaped because he was staying out of Zelda's way. It wasn't a bad strategy.

"Something's wrong with Roger?" asked Grayson.

Zelda's previous approval of Grayson abruptly ended. She rolled her eyes as if indicating that if Grayson had any sense, he would immediately see what was wrong with Roger. "Have you seen his mailbox lately?"

Grayson gave the question careful consideration. "I'm sure I have, but I didn't pay close attention to it."

Zelda waved her hands in the air. "It's horrible! It's not up to the HOA code. Okay, so he wanted to replace his mailbox when he first moved in. Good for him, but he didn't get the standard mailbox for the neighborhood. They're all supposed to be *con-*

sistent. But he put some monstrosity up. I'm sure he's not up to USPS standards for size or height. I'm going to report him."

Quite the welcome to the neighborhood.

Zelda continued. "Then there's his yard art. Have you seen his yard art?"

Grayson and I shook our heads.

"Flamingoes!" she fumed.

I said, "Interesting choice. I didn't realize they were back in fashion."

Zelda muttered. "All different colors. Not just pink."

"Even more of an interesting choice, I said.

"Did you see his wind chimes made from empty beer cans?" demanded Zelda.

I was beginning to think I needed to spend more time on that end of the street. "They sound very whimsical," I offered.

Zelda said darkly, "Changes have gotta be made." Her expression boded ill for Roger Driscoll. "The stuff I have to deal with. Of course, my free dinner at Quittin' Time with Linus tomorrow might be okay." Her expression showed she found that very unlikely.

"It sounds like you've had a rough week," said Grayson. "But the block party is a huge success. Look around—everyone is having a great time. We're all coming together, making connections with our neighbors. It's a really nice event."

Which was when, naturally, everything went horribly wrong. A dog broke away from his owner and merrily ran up and down the street, scarfing down food from every table he passed. Neighbors tried in vain to grab his leash, but the dog was far too fast. The grand finale, before he was finally captured, was when he knocked an entire table of barbeque over and delight-edly gobbled up the spoils of his raid.

Zelda's face was quite a picture. She took another long drag on her cigarette in a futile attempt to steady her nerves. I glanced over at Grayson, wondering how he could put a positive spin on this particular setback. "They've got the dog now," he said cheerfully.

Zelda just glared coldly. Which was when a sudden rain-storm blew in, dumping buckets of rain on us and extinguishing Zelda's cigarette quite effectively.

"Gotta close it all down," she snarled, stomping away. "Last block party!"

Grayson helped me grab my salad, plates, and the table. Al-ready soaking wet, we scrambled for the house.

Chapter Eleven

Safely inside, I said wryly, "You realize you basically jinxed everything by telling Zelda the night was a success."

He grinned at me. "Sorry about that. But it *was* going really well. Up until the last moment, anyway. I'm sure we can persuade Zelda to allow another block party again. Maybe we can form a committee so she doesn't have to take on all the planning."

"But you know Zelda. Even if we did have a committee, she'd still take everything over. She's awful at delegating."

Grayson said, "She's awful at being in a good mood, too. I don't think I've ever seen her even feeling chipper, much less in a sunny mood." He paused. "What did you make of what she said about Veronica?"

I sighed as I patted the salad dry and transferred it to another container. "Well, aside from the fact that she revealed my patron's identity, I thought it was interesting Veronica was so angry with Victor on the day before his death. She'd given me the impression that she hadn't seen him for ages. It sounds like she wasn't exactly being truthful."

Fitz sauntered into the kitchen, regarding us thoughtfully as we dripped rainwater all over the floor. I pulled out a few cat treats and put them in front of him. "It's been a weird evening, hasn't it, Fitz?"

Fitz's expression seemed to agree with me. I rarely pulled furniture into the front yard, stuck food on it, and talked with neighbors. Or got caught in massive rainstorms without an umbrella. He gave up trying to figure it out and happily nibbled his cat treats.

Grayson said, "Okay, so we have a plan for Monday, right? The panel discussion in the community room. If Joel Burns is still as angry at Victor as he had been, it should be easy to get him talking about what went wrong between them."

I nodded. "Hopefully, he'll feel like airing his grievances."

"And you've got the day off tomorrow, right? Feel like hanging out?"

I smiled at him. "Considering you just got that gym membership, I think we'd better make use out of it."

Grayson made a face. "You're right, although the idea of having a very lazy Sunday hanging out in your backyard sounds a lot better somehow."

"Well, if we're going to have weather like this," I said, gesturing to the torrential rain coming down out the window, "then it might be better to be inside doing a workout."

We made plans for Sunday. Grayson grabbed one of my robes, which looked hilariously out-of-place on him, and we threw his soaked clothes in the dryer. Then we curled up together on the sofa to watch *The Maltese Falcon* and drink the wine I'd been wanting earlier.

We did get that workout in on Sunday afternoon, then Grayson and I tried out a group exercise class. It was a body-weight class, which I thought might be an easy way to start out. We were both surprised that the lunges, modified pushups, and squats wore us out as much as they did. "We clearly need this gym membership," said Grayson ruefully.

After the workout, we rewarded ourselves with colorful, healthy smoothies from the café at the gym. The weather cleared up, so we could get the "hanging out time" Grayson had wanted in my backyard, along with some vitamin D from the sunbeams that stretched over the yard.

Monday morning started bright and early for me. Grayson had asked if I wanted to meet up at the gym again before work, but I told him I needed to catch up on a few things around the house before I went to the library. I hadn't been able to get around to doing housework lately, feeling too tired when I got home from work. I emptied the dishwasher and reloaded it, swept and mopped, and wiped down the bathroom. Fitz watched me inquisitively, following me from room to room and leaving little kitty footprints as he padded through the mopped floors. I decided it was his version of floor art and didn't bother to re-mop.

Then we headed off to work, Fitz happily curled up in his carrier. There was nothing I liked better than early mornings at the library. The library always was my happy place, but the mornings were special—the quiet, the sunbeams streaking out from the windows and onto the houseplants we had scattered around the library. And the promise of all those books, all that entertainment and knowledge waiting for me on the shelves.

The quiet continued for a while, even after the library opened to the public. I had a few folks search me out to help them find a particular book. One patron presented me with quite a mystery book . . . they couldn't remember the author, the title, or what genre the book was. They only remembered the cover art. When we found the book, by some miracle, the grin on his face was reward enough.

Around ten-thirty, I started setting up the community room for the mental health panel discussion. Sign-ups for the event had been good, so I pulled out quite a few folding chairs. Grayson came in about fifteen minutes later with a camera and his laptop.

"You're all ready to cover it for the paper," I said.

He nodded, giving me a quick hug in greeting. "After the panel discussion is over, I'll take a few posed pictures, too. Then maybe I can ask Joel if he'll answer a few questions for me for the paper."

Before I could answer, a wave of people came in. I was surprised to see as many as there were. Grayson helped me pull out more chairs. It looked like some people had showed up without registering. That wasn't exactly shocking, as it happened pretty often for library events, but it definitely took me by surprise. Maybe it just went to show the community's interest and concerns about mental health issues.

As soon as Joel Burns came into the room, I recognized him right away. He'd come into the library quite a few times over the years, and I remembered him to be a big reader. He was a middle-aged man with gray hair and a receding hairline. Although I knew he must be about the same age as Victor had been, Joel looked much older. He also looked a little nervous about speaking. Maybe he also hadn't expected as many people in attendance.

The group sponsoring the panel was an office of mental health professionals in town. One of the physicians spoke first, talking about the different areas of mental health that they addressed, which was everything from mood disorders to eating disorders to substance use and addiction. The audience was listening attentively, some people jotting down notes on paper or their phones.

Then the physician turned it over to different folks on the panel. The panel included a licensed therapist, a first responder, a lawyer, and Joel, who was there to talk about his own personal experiences with mental health issues.

Joel might have been nervous when he started speaking, but he quickly became more relaxed as he went along. I could tell that he really wanted to share what he'd gone through, that he wanted to help others to find help instead of just suffering alone. He said, "Mental health isn't' something you really think about, is it? You think things are going to go the way they always have. But when you're going through a lot of stress . . . a failing marriage, job insecurity and loss, and the loss of a friend . . . it can have a tremendous impact on your mental health. Especially if you bring alcohol or other substances into the mix."

The members of the audience were nodding along. They looked even more engaged than they had when the professionals in the field were talking.

Joel continued, "It can be tough to remember that alcohol and drugs aren't going to help anything. They only make things worse in the long run. I'm rebuilding my life after a short stint in rehab. I want to encourage everyone to remember alcoholism and other addictions are diseases just like heart disease or cancer. Seeking help is vital."

The room broke into applause at that. Joel looked surprised, then gratified.

After the talk, no one seemed in any hurry to leave the room. I hung back as small groups of people spoke with the different professionals on the panel. Joel had the most people gathered around him. I was hoping Grayson would have an opportunity to snag him before he left the library.

Fortunately, a few minutes later, people started slowly moving out the door. Grayson immediately asked the remaining panel for a few photos for the paper's article. They were all happy to oblige, considering the entire point of the event was to get the word out about mental health issues and treatment in the area.

After the group photo, Grayson said to Joel, "Would it be okay if I got a few words from you and a separate photo? You did a fantastic job up there relaying your personal experiences."

Joel looked pleased. "Thanks. I was pretty nervous at first."

Grayson waved his hand dismissively. "No one could tell. Anyway, public speaking is everyone's private nightmare."

Grayson took some photos and spoke with Joel for a few minutes, taking down a few notes for his article. All the while, I admired the way Grayson put Joel at ease. He had such an easy manner with everybody. Putting people at ease was definitely not one of my superpowers, but Grayson had it in spades.

After they wrapped up getting material for the paper, I moved in a little closer. "Thanks so much, on behalf of the library, for your part in the panel. I'm sorry you've gone through such a rough time."

Joel said wryly, "Thanks. Sometimes bad luck just doesn't seem like it wants to stop." He glanced around him before saying in a low voice. "Now I've got the police thinking I'm some sort of suspect in what happened a few days ago."

"Victor Sullivan's death?" I asked.

He nodded, regarding me thoughtfully. "As a matter of fact, I believe I heard that one of the librarians had found him. Was that you, by any chance?"

"It was," I said. "I think I remember that the two of you were friends. I'm sorry for your loss."

Joel looked startled for a second, whether from surprise that I knew they'd been friends, or because he hadn't thought of Victor as a friend for a while, I wasn't sure. He said slowly, "Yes, we were friends. But that was a while back." He paused. "I don't suppose I can bend your ear a little, can I? Do you need to get back out front?"

I did, but I needed to clean up the community room first, and there were still plenty of people in it. "No, I'm good."

Joel glanced over at Grayson. "This is all off-the-record, right?"

"Of course," said Grayson.

Joel said, "Sorry, I just had to ask. I don't think I have a very trusting nature anymore, sad to say. My therapist told me I needed to talk more about what I've been experiencing. Some of that is through things like this panel. But some of it needs to be through friendships." He gave a short laugh. "I don't think I'm really ready to take on another friendship yet. But I'm trying to practice what she told me by talking to folks along the way. In a healthy manner, without getting mad."

Grayson and I nodded. I said, "That makes perfect sense."

Joel took a deep breath. "Okay. Well, basically, a lot of my problems started out with Victor. I'm not trying to pin everything on him, though." He stopped himself. "Not true. Maybe I *am* trying to pin everything on him. Right now, he's a pretty tempting scapegoat, especially considering that he's dead. I'm sure the cops think I'm a great suspect because they know I feel that way about Victor."

"How do they know?" asked Grayson.

Joel sighed. "I made a bunch of social media posts, calling Victor out. It was a dumb thing to do, but then I didn't realize Victor was going to end up getting murdered. I was trying to vent my frustration, but it totally backfired on me."

"I know the two of you were good friends. What ended up changing your relationship?" I asked.

Joel paused. "Although I really want to say it's because of Victor, ultimately my therapist has made me realize that I have to shoulder some of the blame, too. But you see, I trusted Victor. We'd been best friends since we were little kids. I would have trusted that guy with my life. But then, I did something stupid and cheated on my wife." He shook his head. "Stupid, like I said. It's one of the biggest regrets of my life. Dena meant everything to me. She was always too good for me. I don't even really know why I did it. I think I was dealing with depression and a lot of unresolved feelings and insecurities. My head was in a bad place."

"And you started a relationship with another woman," said Grayson.

Joel said, "It wasn't a relationship at all. It was a onetime deal. I couldn't believe I'd done it. I was trying to work out in my mind *why* I'd done it. It wasn't anything to do with Dena . . . it was me. So I made another huge mistake and talked to Victor about it."

I said, "That makes sense that you'd reach out to him, though. He was your best friend. Who better to help you work out what was going on with you?"

"Right," said Joel. "That's what I thought, too. I told Victor the very next day. And at first, it seemed like a good idea. Victor had always been a great listener. He had a way of making you feel you're the only person in the world. He'd let you talk for minutes without interrupting, then he'd ask a few pertinent questions that made you realize how well he'd been paying attention. He wouldn't give any advice unless you ask for it."

"Sounds like a great guy," said Grayson.

"Which he was. Until something made him decide to tell Dena that I'd cheated on her." Joel shook his head as if he still couldn't really believe it. "I was stunned."

I said, "Why do you think he did that? Did he offer any kind of explanation?"

"He didn't seem like he would even talk with me about it at first. Of course, I went right over to his office as soon as he was finished with patients and yelled at him and cried for like twenty minutes."

"What did Victor do when you showed up at his office?" I asked.

"Victor just sat in his office chair observing me calmly. Like he was letting me work it out of my system. Finally, once I'd settled down a little, he told me he thought Dena should know. That we wouldn't be able to move forward and have a better future unless we were honest with each other."

Grayson quirked an eyebrow. "So his explanation was that he was helping you fix your relationship? Wasn't that your job?"

"Exactly!" Joel's eyes flared with anger. "Victor could have just given me his opinion as to what he thought I should do and then left it to me to do it. He didn't have to get involved in my business." He shook his head angrily. "Of course, I guess I opened the door to letting him get involved by telling him right away. I should have kept my mouth shut and none of this would have happened."

I said, "Dena didn't take the news well?"

"No. And that's what I regret the most. Every night when I go to sleep, alone, I think of how hurt her eyes were when she told me she knew. How fragile and insecure she seemed. But underneath it all was anger. She filed for divorce right away. She'd grown up with a mom who'd cheated on her dad and she'd sworn to herself that she'd never put up with infidelity like her dad did."

Grayson said, "And you held Victor responsible for your divorce."

"Yeah. I mean, I held myself responsible, too. But I'd never have said a word to Victor if I'd known he was going to tell Dena. I was furious . . . I'm not going to lie. Like I said, the cops have a treasure trove of angry social media posts from me."

"Did you confront Victor in person about it?" I asked.

Joel shook his head. "Not after that first time when I showed up at his office after-hours. My method of dealing with having my wife leave me and my best friend betray me was to drink myself silly and freeze Victor out. It took me a long time to realize I'd had to pay the piper for what I'd done. I never should have strayed from Dena. But I kept thinking it was so hypocritical of Victor to tell Dena. After all, Victor had been the 'other man' in his relationship with Cheryl, who was Roger Driscoll's wife."

I nodded. The whole thing seemed surprising to me, and out of character from what I'd heard about Victor. But then, Victor seemed like he'd been a man of contradictions. He was the beloved doctor who took time with his patients. He betrayed his best friend's confidences. He listened to all his patients' concerns. He was tough on staff at his office. Maybe it was just a sign that he'd been a complex man who was hard to get a full picture of.

Joel continued. "I can't blame Dena for leaving me. Right now, I'm working with my therapists to focus on all the good times we had. Our divorce didn't erase those. It wasn't like we were living a lie." He gave another short laugh. "At least, that's what my therapist keeps telling me. Dena and I had a lot in common. We met in college and both worked hard. I went into insurance and Dena was a banker. We both were at school with Victor. I was never as ambitious as Victor was, but I was always pulling for him."

We were quiet for a moment. Then Grayson said, "It seems like you went through just a really dark time. You've pulled yourself out of it, too."

"With the help of a bunch of professionals," said Joel wryly.

"If the police could focus on another suspect, that would take some of the pressure off of you," said Grayson. "Do you have any idea who might have been that angry with Victor?"

"Besides me, you mean? Well, there were a few people. I know that's hard to believe. Sometimes, I felt like I was the only person in the world who didn't think Victor walked on water. One of them is Veronica Carpenter. She blamed Victor for malpractice in her husband's death."

I nodded. Joel didn't seem surprised that I'd already heard about Veronica. He continued. "Then there's the people he used to work with. Victor and I were close enough that he used to blow off steam with me after a day at the office. I always got the impression that Victor was great with his patients and much harder on his staff and colleagues."

"Was there anyone in particular that Victor didn't get along well with?" I asked."

"Victor had some kind of trouble with Dr. Lee. One night, we were talking on the back porch after a little too much wine. Victor said that Dr. Lee was doing something she shouldn't be doing."

Grayson said slowly, "Did Victor say what it was?"

"He didn't elaborate," said Joel. "But I didn't think it was related to patient safety or anything like that. That's all I know." He added, "I also don't think he liked that medical student over there."

"Did you talk to Victor about that?" I asked.

"No, that was after he and I had ended our friendship. But I heard from a mutual friend of ours that Victor thought the kid couldn't handle criticism. Victor thought he was one of those guys who'd always been told how great he was and had totally bought into that. He thought he was God's gift to medicine and that he already knew everything he needed to know. The kid couldn't stand being corrected."

It sounded likely. I had definitely gotten the impression that Kyle was cocky.

The last few people in the room filed out. Joel said, "I better get going. Off-the-record," he said, wagging a finger at Grayson again.

"You have my word," said Grayson.

Chapter Twelve

We had the room to ourselves. Grayson gave me a hand, putting the folding chairs away. He said, "What did you make of Joel?"

"He did a great job with his panel. I think he went through quite a journey, losing everything before working to find himself again." I hesitated. "I wasn't sure what to make of his thoughts on Victor."

Grayson nodded. "They didn't seem to gel with what we'd been hearing about Dr. Sullivan, did they?"

"Right. I guess Victor wasn't as simple to read as everybody seemed to think. Maybe he had something of a dark side." I shrugged. "Or maybe his conscience was bothering him and he knew he couldn't be around Joel's wife and pretend he didn't know Joel was cheating on her. Who knows?"

Grayson said, "Like Joel was saying, it was pretty ironic that Victor would suddenly develop a conscience. After all, he broke up Roger Driscoll's marriage. Then we have Paige Lee. I'd like to find out more about this problem that Victor found out about Dr. Lee. Do you think he knew she'd acted unethically or something like that?"

"I don't know. If she did, maybe she decided it would be safer to shut Victor up permanently. He doesn't seem like he'd have been the sort to blackmail anybody." I was quiet for a moment. "Then we've got Kyle Bowman again."

Grayson smirked. "It doesn't sound like Victor was very impressed with him."

"No. And I can attest to the fact that Kyle thinks a lot of himself. Did I tell you he'd asked me out when I saw him in the library the other day?"

"The nerve," said Grayson in a teasing voice. "I hope you gave him a bloody nose."

"I showed admirable restraint," I said, smiling back at him. "The thing was, it wasn't even like I felt special that he'd singled me out. I'd heard the guy ask one of our patrons out a few weeks ago. I think he just enjoys feeding his ego."

"Well, hopefully, your refusal took him down a notch." Grayson glanced at his watch regretfully. "I can't pretend I have any further business at the library, unfortunately. I'd better head back to the newsroom and check on how tomorrow's edition is coming together."

"Good luck with it," I said.

That afternoon, I started thinking about what I'd heard from Joel after the panel. I decided I'd better give Burton a call and clue him in. I wasn't sure if anything I'd learned was important, but I figured I'd better be on the safe side.

"Ann," he said, immediately picking up my call. "Is everything going okay?"

I gave a wry smile. Considering what had happened on Friday, Burton was probably worried that I'd discovered yet another body. "It's all good. I just wanted to check in with you and give you a snippet of information that I have. Is now a good time?"

"Sure," he said. I could hear him walking away from a noisy location in search of something quieter. "Go ahead."

"I'm not totally convinced that this is something you don't already know," I said, starting out with a disclaimer.

"Doesn't matter," said Burton. "See something, say something."

"This is more a case of 'hear something, say something.' I spoke with Joel Burns this morning at the library."

"Joel? Victor's former friend, right? We've talked to him a couple of times. He definitely seemed like he had a decent motive to get rid of Victor."

"Yeah, I had the feeling you were probably considering him a person of interest. He was saying Victor told him one night, when they were still friends, that Victor knew Paige Lee was doing something she shouldn't be doing. I thought I should just pass that along to you."

Burton said, "Got it. Well, I appreciate the insight. I'm not really sure what to make of it, though. After talking to the staff over at the clinic, I learned Victor had a habit of making mountains out of molehills. It sounded like he took the same angle with the medical student."

"Victor was blowing things out of proportion?"

Burton said, "Totally. The team found an email from a couple of months ago on Victor's personal laptop with a list of grievances against Dr. Lee. I have to say it was petty stuff."

"You know they used to date, right?"

Burton said, "Yeah, the nurses clued us into that, too. Not real appropriate for work, of course. The nurses weren't happy at all about it. Seems like, when those two were dating, they got along even *worse* with each other than they had before. They couldn't wait for them to break things off. And it sounds like it wasn't too long after that when they ended the relationship."

"So you think the list of grievances might be because Victor was soured on Dr. Lee because of their bad relationship?" I asked.

"Could be. I mean, it really was petty. Dr. Lee took office supplies home for personal use. She left patient files on her desk, which Victor thought was careless. She took longer-than-allowed breaks and used her personal phone too often during work hours. Just minor stuff."

I said, "Yeah, that doesn't sound like much. Maybe whatever Joel was talking about was more of the same—Victor making something out of nothing."

"Well, keep your ears open, Ann. I appreciate you filling me in. Who knows? Maybe something will come of it." Someone called his name in the background, and Burton said, "Gotta go. Thanks again, Ann." And he hung up.

Fitz, who'd been sprawled out in front of me on the reference desk, suddenly perked up and rose. I smiled when I saw Linus coming up. Fitz had a real soft spot for my senior patron, and the feeling seemed to be returned. "He saw you coming," I said to Linus as Fitz bumped Linus's hand with his head.

Linus scratched Fitz under his chin, smiling as Fitz closed his eyes happily. "My library friend," said Linus to the cat.

"Hey, I wanted to ask you how everything went last night at the dinner with Zelda?" I asked.

Linus smiled. "It was actually a very pleasant evening. I'm glad I took your advice and didn't get her a corsage. That would have been overkill. You're right—she definitely didn't consider our dinner a date at all. She wore casual clothes, but looked very nice."

Linus was always a gentleman. I had the feeling Zelda might have shown up for dinner in one of her usual outfits. Perhaps the no-nonsense wrinkle-free black pants, paired with a plaid top.

He continued, "I'd actually only been there once, for lunch at that. But then, I'm something of a creature of habit and used to eating at home. I thought the restaurant had lots of charm, with its vintage décor, checkerboard tablecloths, and the open kitchen."

I tried to recall the vintage décor he was talking about. I did remember some old photos and newspaper clippings on the wall. When I thought harder, I recalled a small collection of vinyl records hanging on the walls, and antique signs with quirky slogans.

"It was so busy there. I was grateful Zelda had thought ahead and made a reservation. I don't think we'd have gotten a seat if she hadn't."

I hadn't been aware that Quittin' Time, a spur-of-the-moment type of dining establishment, even accepted reservations. Perhaps Zelda had forced them into it.

Linus continued, "It was surprising that a Sunday night would be that busy. But it was a great restaurant. It had such a warm and welcoming atmosphere."

"What did you order?" I asked.

"Well, I had a tough time deciding between entrees. After Zelda recommended the burger, I ordered that. Delicious! It had a perfectly grilled patty and a delicate balance of seasonings. The potato salad it came with was simply amazing. It reminded me of the potato salad my mother made when I was just a lad. The meal also came with a side of garlic toast, which complemented it perfectly."

I said, "I'm so glad it was good. Did you have a difficult time coming up with conversation with Zelda?"

"That's the biggest surprise of all. Usually, I'm a bit shy when it comes to speaking with someone I don't know well. But Zelda was actually quite an interesting conversationalist."

I was starting to wonder if he'd really been eating with Zelda or if she'd sent a doppelgänger as a substitute. "Really? What did you talk about?" Because from my many conversations with Zelda, they seemed to be focused on HOA infractions, irritating library patrons, and other sources of dismay for Zelda.

"Well, we talked a bit about neuroscience and how it intersected with creative expression. Zelda had some fascinating thoughts on that," said Linus. "She's quite the documentary viewer, apparently. She said that engaging in creative pursuits stimulates neuroplasticity."

I blinked. "Remind me again what neuroplasticity is?"

"Oh, it's just the brain's ability to form new neural connections. It's basically the brain's way of reorganizing itself."

Linus wasn't the type of person to pull my leg. But it was very difficult to reconcile my Zelda with the Zelda who went to dinner with him.

Linus said, "Ethics in technology was another conversation. Especially relating to privacy concerns, ethical hacking, and digital rights."

"Wow," I said. I was blown away.

"Even if we *had* run out of conversation, which wasn't going to happen, the band that played last night was truly wonderful. It comprised a very talented lead singer and two excellent band members. It was an enjoyable evening. We decided it would be nice to have coffees from time to time, perhaps when Zelda leaves from a volunteer shift. We seemed to have a good deal in common."

Linus gave Fitz a final rub and said, "I'd better let you get back to work. Thanks again to the library for the free meal."

"Anytime you want to come and win trivia night again, feel free." Although it sounded as if Zelda might give him a run for his money again.

The next morning, I woke up blissfully late. At least, it felt late because I'd been getting up so early the last few work days. But this was my day off and lateness felt wonderful.

I sat up in bed and saw Fitz was already sitting in the doorway, looking at me a bit reproachfully. "Sorry, Fitz. I know—this establishment has very poor service. And yet, you keep frequenting this restaurant, don't you?"

Fitz looked a lot more cheerful when I clambered out of bed and headed toward the kitchen. He wound himself around my legs as I got out a clean bowl and filled it with wet cat food. It always smelled revolting to me, especially first thing in the morning, but Fitz seemed to love it. As he gobbled it up, I turned on the coffeepot and stumbled off to take a shower. It was Tuesday, and I knew Grayson would already be at the office. That meant there was really no hurry to get ready for anything—we had no plans or any agenda. In many ways, this was a disappointment. But I had to admit that, in some small way, it felt delicious to have a whole day to do whatever I felt like.

While I got ready, I mulled over the different ways to spend my Tuesday. I could take a hike. I could just snuggle with Fitz on the sofa and read my book. I was finally getting around to reading *The Silent Patient* by Alex Michaelides after hearing patrons sing its praises for years. So far, it was a really solid read. And, of course, the medical theme seemed to fit in eerily well with Victor's death.

Thinking about books, though, also reminded me of something else. I'd promised myself that I'd do a better job with my book collection. I glanced around the house. Books were in overflowing bookcases, stacked on end tables, and even neatly piled against a couple of walls. It was very, very hard for me to get rid of books, even though I knew I could check out any book I wanted to read from the library. Maybe it was because my own personal library brought back so many memories—mostly of my great aunt, who'd raised me and had been a huge booklover, herself.

I decided if I made just the slightest amount of progress, I'd consider the day a success. I remembered there were a couple of Little Free Libraries that weren't too far away. Maybe I'd take a handful of books and divide them up between the two. I'd resist the temptation to take a book *out* of the Little Free Libraries (easier said than done). Then I could come back home, make myself something to eat, and snuggle up with Fitz.

Winnowing out the handful of books was a longer process than I'd anticipated. Only one pick was easy . . . a duplicate copy of a book. It didn't help that I found myself lost down a rabbit hole when I picked up books, leafed through them, and then started reading a few of my favorite passages. Finally, I set myself a timer on my phone and sternly told myself to get down to business. Twenty minutes later, I had a modest selection to give away.

I stroked Fitz, telling him I'd be back soon. Then I hopped into my aging Subaru and drove to one of the two free libraries. At the first one, I deposited three books and managed not to take a copy of *Bird by Bird*, an excellent homage to the writing life by Anne Lamott. Then I headed off to the second free library location.

This neighborhood was one of Whitby's older ones, with mature trees, wide sidewalks, and a mix of Craftsman, Victorian, and Colonial Revival architecture. As I drove up to the small wooden library near the sidewalk, I saw the glare of lights from emergency vehicles ahead. I frowned. I knew it was probably just a medical emergency and had nothing to do with the murder investigation. But after I put my books in the little library, I parked my car and walked down the street toward the lights, feeling pulled there.

Burton was outside, speaking with police officers from the state police. I hung back, watching the scene. Burton spotted me after a few minutes and motioned me over.

"What's going on?" I asked quietly.

"It's Kyle Bowman," said Burton in a grim voice. "We found him dead in his Airbnb."

Chapter Thirteen

"Murder?" I asked, although I was sure it must be. Kyle didn't seem to be the kind to want to inflict any self-harm.

Burton nodded. "He didn't show up for work this morning, which was apparently really unusual. From what I heard, he likes to come in first thing. Kyle also didn't pick up his phone when work tried calling him. Dr. Lee phoned us up and asked us to do a wellness check."

"Can I ask what the weapon was?"

Burton said, "Sure, if you make sure it doesn't go any further. A dumbbell from a makeshift workout area Kyle had set up." He glanced behind me as a car drove up. "Looks like Dr. Lee is going to join us."

I turned to see a Mercedes pull up to the sidewalk to park. Dr. Lee quickly stepped out of her car, looking very pale. I noticed that she appeared a lot more shaken this time than she had over Victor's death. She wrung her hands together nervously as she hurried up to us.

"He's dead?" she asked, before even coming all the way up to us. "Kyle?"

"I'm afraid so," Burton said.

She briefly closed her eyes. "What's happening? He was just a kid."

Burton said, "When was the last time you spoke with him?"

"Yesterday evening, at work. We had a busy Monday at the office. No surprise with that, of course. Mondays tend to be busy because we have limited weekend hours. Plus, with Victor being gone, Kyle and I were handling a higher workload."

Dr. Lee almost made it sound as if Victor was away on vacation. Maybe she just had a gift for compartmentalizing. Again, I found it tough to imagine the two of them in a relationship with each other.

She continued. "We saw our last patients, then we had our wrap-up to evaluate how the day had gone . . . successes, challenges, that sort of thing. It's something I like to do with medical students. Instead of putting the day behind them, it can be helpful for them to reflect on what went right or wrong, and learn from the experience."

Burton nodded, taking some notes. "What time was that?"

Dr. Lee thought for a minute. "Off the top of my head, we were doing our wrap-up at about seven o'clock. We probably finished up with our last patients around six-thirty."

Burton lifted his brows. "Although the clinic closes at five?"

"That's right. It was a busy day, as I mentioned."

Burton said, "What was Kyle's demeanor during this wrap-up of yours?"

Dr. Lee gave a small snort. "His demeanor? He wanted to get out of there. Kyle was impatient and wanted to go home."

"Did you get the impression that he wanted to get home to rest after a long day?" asked Burton.

"I didn't get *any* impression from him. I was simply doing my job and reviewing the medical end of things. If Kyle had plans or something he wanted to do after work, he didn't share those with me, and I didn't ask."

Burton asked, "Was Kyle ordinarily like that? Ready to get out of work?"

"Well, ordinarily it would have been Victor with him, of course, so I'm not really privy to that information." She paused. "I do recall Kyle being very impatient to leave, however. There was one day in particular that comes to mind. Kyle was waiting for Victor to wrap things up with a patient. I thought the young man was going to pop out of his skin, he was so agitated. He told me Victor was taking forever, and that he hated having to wait for him. He had pure frustration coming out of him."

Burton nodded. "I remember hearing Victor took a long time with his patients." He suddenly switched his line of questioning, perhaps hoping to catch Paige Lee off-balance. "Could you account for your actions last night and early this morning?"

His tactic worked. Dr. Lee grew even paler, and she put a protective hand up to her neck. "You can't think I had anything to do with Kyle's death? Why would I do something like that?"

"It's just standard procedure," said Burton evenly.

Dr. Lee hesitated. "Well, after I drove back from the clinic, I changed, then went out for a run, like I always do. After that, it was getting dark, so I went home to make myself some supper. I turned in around nine o'clock since I was fairly exhausted from the day. I slept hard until the alarm went off this morning. Then I went into the office."

I noticed she sounded a lot less flippant in her recital of her movements than she had after Victor's death.

"You know the rest; when Kyle didn't show up, we all became concerned," said Dr. Lee quietly.

Burton nodded. "You said he was usually prompt."

"He was all about making a good impression. If anything, he was ordinarily early. He could be the first person at the practice." She was quiet for a few moments. "Kyle had his issues, of course. He needed to learn patience, for one." She took a deep breath that shook a little. Maybe that was because she realized he wasn't going to learn patience, after all. She kept going. "And he was overconfident in his abilities. But he wanted to do a good job, and he was a reliable employee. We knew at once that something must be wrong when he didn't arrive at the clinic." She put a hand up to her head and rubbed her temple. "I'll have to tell his parents. They're going to be devastated."

Before Burton could reply or ask another question, Dr. Lee said, "I'm concerned that we've now lost two of our medical providers in the last week. I've had to reschedule our morning's patients. I know it's horrible of me to be concerned about business implications at a time like this, but should the staff and I be worried? It's almost as if someone is targeting providers at our clinic. Do I need to get security at the building? What's going on? You *must* make progress on this investigation."

Her voice rose at the end and a flush moved over her pale features. This was likely about as wound up as Dr. Lee got.

Burton noted the change, too. "I don't believe any extraordinary precautions need to be made. I can send a deputy over if that would make you feel better."

She nodded, looking relieved. "Yes. Yes, I think that would help."

"I'll get somebody there for the next couple of days. But again, I don't really think you or the staff need to be worried. Just be careful coming and going from the parking lot. That's always a good idea, regardless of the circumstances."

Before Dr. Lee could continue, Burton said, "Have you thought any more about Victor's death? Gotten any insights as to what happened? I know we've been focusing on Kyle's death, but I can't help feeling the two must be related."

She gave a short laugh. "I don't think you realize how very crazy it's been at the clinic since Victor's death. The receptionists are losing their minds trying to reschedule patients and send medical records to patients who want to change practices. Kyle and I have been trying to handle our own patients and Victor's, too. So, no, I haven't spent much time thinking about Victor's death."

"That's understandable," Burton said. "It's just that I've been hearing reports that you and Victor didn't get along as well as you said you had. And that you were formerly in a relationship. That wasn't something you mentioned the first time you and I spoke."

Dr. Lee pressed her lips together tightly for a moment. I could tell her brain was spinning, trying to find a reasonable explanation for failing to divulge that information. Finally she said, "I didn't think mentioning our former relationship would make any difference. It was irrelevant whether or not we'd dated in the past."

"Unfortunately, in a murder investigation, most things are relevant. That kind of information provides background and context for us."

She bobbed her head. "I see. I'm sorry I didn't mention it." She paused. "I'll admit Victor and I weren't similar personalities. Perhaps opposites attracted in that instance. Our relationship was very short and rather uninspired. We were clearly not suited to each other."

Burton said suddenly, "During the course of the investigation, we found evidence Victor was angry or irritated with you."

Dr. Lee suddenly became very still. "What do you mean?"

Burton said, "We found emails showing Victor was displeased about your taking office supplies home, and that sort of thing."

Dr. Lee's eyes flashed with irritation, although she seemed to relax somewhat. "Oh, he could be ridiculous with that kind of thing. He knew half the time when I was at home, I was still making notes and doing work. Why *shouldn't* I take a legal pad home?"

"He also seemed to take issue with your use of the phone during work hours."

Dr. Lee said, "More nonsense. I was simply more adept at handling my schedule. Therefore, I had more free time. One way I could shake off the pressure at the office was to scroll through social media. I'll freely admit it's a waste of time, but it helped me relax during those tiny pockets of time I'd get during the day. Victor was always really exacting and fastidious about work being work. While you're at work, in Victor's world, you were never taking a break."

Burton raised his brows again. "Never? What about lunch?"

"That was another point of contention between us. I believe employees perform better when they work their time efficiently for self-care. We'd clash over this idea sometimes. But then, we spent many hours a day with each other. I deeply disliked having my professional life put under a microscope. I was doing my job and doing it well. If I was doing it differently than Victor, that was my business."

Burton nodded, making a few more notes. "Can you tell me a little about your professional relationship with Kyle? I know you mentioned he was overconfident."

"He was. But that's not a crime. If it was, then most med school students would be incarcerated," she said with a small smile. "You have to have a certain amount of self-confidence to even get this far in the process."

Burton said, "The last time we spoke, you mentioned you believed Kyle could have been responsible for Victor's death."

"Well, that seems a little unlikely now, doesn't it? I'll retract that suspicion of mine. But yes, I'd honestly believed he had the ability to lash out at Victor. Like I mentioned earlier, he could get quite frustrated with him. Kyle was young and brash. But that didn't make him a killer, clearly." She paused. "Have you spoken to that former patient of Victor's?"

"Veronica? Or was there another?" asked Burton.

"Veronica. Maybe you need to double-down on talking to her. She's such an intense person and unrelenting in her anger against Victor. That had to count for something. Perhaps she just got caught up in the moment and her feelings and murdered Victor." She looked irritated. "But that's just speculation on my part. It's your job to figure out what happened."

One of the state police officers called Burton's name. He turned and nodded to the officer before turning back to Dr. Lee. "Okay. I may need to speak with you again, so just a heads-up on that. But you can head back to the clinic if you need to."

Dr. Lee acknowledged this with a stiff nod of her head before walking swiftly back to the Mercedes.

"I'll see you later, Ann." And Burton hurried away, too.

Chapter Fourteen

I drove slowly back home, thinking about Kyle all the way. When I got home, Fitz picked up on my mood again and leaned his furry body against my leg as soon as I came in. I picked him up and buried my face in his fluffiness. He bumped his head against mine, looking lovingly into my eyes.

"It's been another crazy morning," I said to him. Fitz gazed at me in an understanding manner.

I set down the cat and absently made myself something light to eat. Then I phoned Grayson.

"I think your day is about to take a detour," I said grimly.

"Why? What's happened? Are you okay?"

I said, "I'm fine. But Kyle Bowman is dead. Murdered at home."

I could hear movement on the other end of the phone. "You're right. My day is taking a detour. Thanks for letting me know. You're sure you're okay?"

"I'm good. I didn't find him—the police were doing a wellness check when he didn't show up for work this morning," I said.

"I'll give Burton a call. And maybe see if I can get a quote from Paige Lee." I could tell his mind was already going a million miles an hour, planning the story.

"I'll talk to you later. Hope you get everything you need for the article."

Grayson said, "What are your plans for the day?"

"Well, I was thinking I would curl up with Fitz and read my book. But I'm probably too keyed up right now to get that done. Maybe I'll work some more on housework or do something in the yard."

Grayson said, "There's always the gym, too."

"Right. I'd forgotten about that." I wasn't used to having a gym membership. But now that Grayson had mentioned it, a trip to the gym was sounding very appealing. That would definitely be the way to work off the excess energy I was feeling. "That might just fit the bill. I'll talk to you later, Grayson."

I changed into workout clothes and took off for the gym. It was busier than it had been the last time I was there, but there was still plenty of equipment for me to exercise on. I decided I wasn't in the right mood for a group class, so I headed straight for the weights, then the treadmill.

By the time I left the gym, I did feel better. My head felt clearer, for sure, and I felt like I was ready to make a plan for the rest of my day. I definitely wanted to get my reading time in, but it made more sense for me to do that yard work first, since I was already sweaty from my workout.

So after getting home, I gave Fitz a few rubs as he was happily lying in a sunbeam, then grabbed a pair of gardening gloves, a bucket to dump weeds in, and some pruners, and headed outside.

Although yardwork wasn't my favorite thing to do, it definitely gave me the same sense of satisfaction that housework did. Basically, it was just good to knock stuff off my list and see the before-and-after effects of what I'd accomplished.

Unfortunately, I managed to stir up pollen in my efforts to tidy the yard. This resulted in a huge sneezing and coughing fit. Hearing me, Fitz leaped up into the window, watching me with alarm. I hurried inside to take my allergy medicine and drink a glass of water, as Fitz regarded me with concern.

Five minutes later, I was pulling up a patch of clover that had implanted itself when I heard a cheery voice say, "Hi there, neighbor."

I stood, brushing dirt off my clothes, and saw Roger Driscoll standing there. "Hey, Roger. How's it going? You've got the day off, too?"

"I decided it was time for me to take a personal health day. Plus, I pulled something on the job yesterday." He rubbed his shoulder, then gingerly rotated it, wincing. "One of the hazards of construction life." He smiled at me. "I guess you don't have those kinds of problems where you work. Actually, I can't remember where you work."

"I'm a librarian," I said with a smile. Half the time when I disclosed this, I was armed and ready for various librarian jokes. But Roger either didn't know them or didn't seem inclined to make them.

"Nice work," he said. He sounded a little wistful. "You won't believe this, but when I was a kid, I thought I might work around books. A bookstore, a library. Something like that. My sister and I even 'played library.' We'd pretend to check out books, stock shelves. That kind of thing."

"That all sounds very familiar," I said. "So what happened to your dream of working with books?"

"Oh, that was just the first of a long line of me choosing different future jobs. Then I wanted to be an archaeologist, an astronaut, and a vet. Finally, I went with what I was best at . . . working with my hands, figuring out how to put things together." He shrugged. "It's been a good life." He gestured to the garden. "Looks like you know something about gardening, too. I guess, if you're a librarian, you might know a lot about tons of stuff."

"I guess it comes with the job. Not that I know everything, but patrons ask me questions about topics, and I find out more about them through research. But I can't really take the credit for this garden. It's courtesy of my great-aunt, who raised me."

Roger nodded. "Got it. You know, the new place has a pretty nice garden. I've thought about taking up gardening through the years. Maybe even making a side-gig out of doing yardwork for other people. But when I was out in the yard this morning, I didn't know what some of those plants even were. Do you think you could help me identify them? I could take pictures of them to show you."

"Have you tried doing a reverse Google image search? You could probably find out right away what the plants are and how to care for them," I said.

Roger shook his head. "I don't know how to do that, but it sounds useful."

I said, "It can be. You pull up a Google search, hit the camera icon next to the search box, and take a photo. Then Google looks for a match online. I can show you how to do it."

"No, that's too much trouble right now. You're in gardening mode. Maybe I'll run by the library sometime and ask you then." He paused, looking at the yard again. "I really like those plants you've got there. Are they lilies?"

"Daylilies," I said. "They're pretty, aren't they? Would you like some of them?"

Roger immediately started shaking his head. "I don't want you to pull up any of your plants."

"I wouldn't have to. Daylilies can be divided at the root. Besides, these really do need to be divided to give them some breathing room. I've been putting it off."

"Only if you can spare them. And only if you have time at some point. I think they'd look good around my mailbox."

I hid a smile. I supposed this was the monstrous mailbox that Zelda complained about.

Roger was quiet for a few moments. "Hey, I was wondering if you heard all those sirens earlier. Do you know anything about that? It seemed like a lot more sirens than there would be for a regular medical emergency."

I said, "I'm afraid it was another murder. Kyle Bowman died. He was a medical student who was working at the clinic for one of his rotations."

Roger looked shocked. "You're kidding. What's going on? Was it the same clinic where Victor worked?"

I nodded, and Roger shook his head. "This is getting insane. Does somebody have some sort of vendetta against doctors or something?"

I shook my head. "I don't have any idea. I'm just guessing that the two murders are connected somehow."

Roger sighed. "Crud. This is going to mean a return visit from the police, I bet. That's not going to be fun for my day off."

"No alibi, I guess?" I asked.

"Nope. I was at home, sleeping in this morning. It happened this morning, right?"

I said, "I don't know for sure. It sounded like the police were asking people about their last twelve hours or so."

"Well, last night I went to bed early after I fell asleep watching TV on the sofa. I guess the cops won't think that's much of an alibi. But I don't know this Kyle person. I've heard of him, but never met him. That should be a good reason for me not to be a suspect." He ran a hand through his unbrushed gray hair. "I can't believe I'm getting yanked into this investigation. And this all happened when I'm trying to move forward and get past everything."

I gave him an encouraging look, and Roger continued. "I was thinking yesterday about what I was saying to you and Grayson at the block party. My dad always told me when I was growing up that I could get bitter or better. I never had anything to get bitter about until Victor and Cheryl got together, but then I made up for lost time. I've been stuck for a while and I realized I needed to find a way to pull myself out of it."

"What are you planning on doing?" I asked.

Roger said, "To start out, I'm going to go to Victor's funeral. I want it to be like a new beginning for me. And, maybe, I want Cheryl and other people in town to realize that I have the ability to put the past behind me. After that, I'm going to focus more on my health. Cut back on drinking, try to eat a vegetarian meal or two in a week."

"Sounds like a great plan."

He smiled at me. "Thanks. I figure if I can just focus on me instead of worrying about other people and how they've wronged me, I should get my head in a better place." He sighed. "If I can. It seems like this murder investigation is determined to drag me back into the past again."

"I know last time you were thinking Joel Burns might have had something to do with Victor's death. Is that still what you're thinking?"

Roger shook his head. "See, that's part of the mindset that I need to fix. Trying to blame other people all the time. I like Joel, and we used to be buddies. I feel bad about throwing him under the bus for Victor's murder. I just haven't seen the guy for a while. There's really nothing about Joel that makes me feel like he could have done something like that to Victor."

I said, "Life gets so busy that sometimes it's easy to let friendships fall by the wayside."

"Yeah, but it shouldn't be that way. I've just been so caught up with all the bad stuff going on in my life that I haven't kept up with friends like I should have. That's on me. I'm going to try to do better. The fact is, Joel went through a rough time, too. He also lost a marriage. Then he ended up with addiction issues. He could have used a friend, but I was off sulking. Maybe I'll reach out to him and we can grab a coffee today."

I said, "I saw Joel recently, and he was looking great."

"I'm glad to hear that," said Roger, sounding like he meant it. "That's actually really inspiring, that he was able to lift himself out of where he'd been. Because I think he'd been in a very dark place." He gave me a smile. "Well, thanks for the chat. I better let you get back to your yardwork."

"Thanks. I'll run those daylilies by soon."

Roger said, "No hurry on that. But thank you." He frowned, glanced swiftly down the street and said, "I'd better run. Talk to you later."

I glanced curiously to see who might have caused him to flee like that, and saw, naturally, it was Zelda, stomping down the street. He must have wanted to avoid any conversations pertaining to inappropriate mailboxes and questionable yard art.

Ordinarily, I'd have tried to avoid Zelda too, but she'd already spotted me. She bared her teeth in a smile. "Hi, Ann."

"How's everything going, Zelda?"

"Better than it's going to go for that Roger Driscoll when I catch him. The man is avoiding me."

I said, "I think he was in a hurry to run an errand or something."

Zelda growled, "He'll have to be around at some point. Then I'll tell him a thing or two."

Wanting to get off the subject before Zelda really started getting warmed up on HOA violations, I quickly said, "How did the free dinner at Quittin' Time go?"

Zelda grunted. Then she said, "Okay, I guess."

It was hardly a rave review. "Did you run into any problems redeeming the meal?"

"No, nothing like that," she said. "But you know. It was Quittin' Time."

"Sadly, we don't have a whole lot of choices around Whitby," I said.

Zelda looked tempted to go off on a tangent about that very problem, but managed to restrain herself.

"The clientele isn't great, either," she said with a sniff. "It's a real mixed bag. This woman at the table next to me was wearing a perfume that gave me a headache. Too strong! You'd think people would be aware of that."

"That can be awful," I acknowledged. "Lots of people are allergic to scents, too."

Zelda appeared not to be concerned about the other people. She shrugged a thin shoulder. "Linus asked me what he should get, and I told him the burger, since it was the safest thing on the menu. If they try to cook fancy food at Quittin' Time, that's when stuff goes wrong."

"Fancy?" I couldn't imagine what might qualify as fancy food on their menu.

Zelda barked, "Quiche! Beef stroganoff!"

I nodded, because she clearly required agreement. "But the burger was good?"

"Acceptable," she said shortly. "I had to ask them to modify it, of course, and they messed that all up. I told them to put the pickle on the side, and they didn't. I told them I didn't want any of that brioche bun nonsense. I wanted a sesame seed bun, toasted but not too crispy. I wanted cheddar cheese on top, but not dripping off the side. The lettuce needed to be crisp and the tomato fresh."

I had the funny feeling that Zelda's burger hadn't come out exactly as she ordered it.

Zelda scowled. "It was all a mess. A mess! Nothing the way it was supposed to be."

I was still trying to look for a silver lining. "But there was a live band, though, right? I know they usually have them."

"They were atrocious. The music was too loud and the singer couldn't sing to save her soul."

I finally decided that perhaps it would be best for Zelda to find the bright spot in the evening. "Did anything go right?"

Zelda reflected on this. She said grudgingly, "Linus was a real gentleman. He was always holding doors, pulling out my chair for me to sit, helped me with my coat. Nice guy. And real interesting." She paused. "Guess it's all those books he's reading."

Zelda, despite her interest in shelving books and hanging out at the library, was not much of a reader. It was extraordinary to me that she was as good at trivia as she was.

Zelda continued, "Yeah, we had real interesting conversations. He asked me a lot of questions, too. He thought it was intriguing that I knew so much about mythology."

"How *do* you know so much about mythology?" I asked. Again, because I'd seen no evidence that Zelda had ever read a book of mythology.

She shrugged. "My parents. They told me the stories. Smart folks."

"What did they do?" I asked.

"Dad was an English professor, and Mom was an archaeologist."

The conversation with Zelda was getting more and more surprising as it went on. "I had no idea," I said slowly. I kept feeling as if I'd walked through the looking glass.

Zelda glowered at me. "You can't know if you don't ask. Anyway, Linus was nice. We don't want to romance each other, but he's great. I wouldn't mind chewing the fat with him another time." She was quiet for a few moments. "Of course, he did show up looking like he was about to cut the ribbon at a bank opening."

I smiled. "He's pretty attached to his suit and tie."

"It stands out a little at Quittin' Time. Maybe I can work on that." Then she said gruffly, "Those hydrangeas need trimming," and stomped away.

Chapter Fifteen

The rest of Tuesday went quietly. I got cleaned up and got that reading time in with Fitz. After that, I turned on the TV and lazily flipped through channels, but saw nothing I found interesting enough to spend time on. Then I read some more until I finished the book. I jotted down a few notes, thinking it might make an excellent selection for the library's book club.

Grayson came over in a surprise visit at six o'clock. He tapped lightly at my front door and held up two takeout bags, grinning, when I opened the door. "Did I catch you before you cooked anything?"

I reached out and gave him a hug. "You must have read my mind. I was definitely *not* planning on cooking anything. I was actually trying to decide between honey oat cereal and frozen pancakes."

He set the bags of food down on the kitchen table. "Hopefully, this will be better than either of those. The very best menu items that Quittin' Time offers."

"Let me see. Those must be the fried chicken platter and their smoked brisket."

Grayson said, "And two slices of their pecan pie. I almost got an entire pie, but I thought that might be overkill."

"Speaking of the restaurant, Linus and Zelda gave me their accounts, separately, of how their complementary dinner at Quittin' Time went."

Grayson raised an eyebrow. "You could tell me anything, and I wouldn't be surprised."

"I still think you might be able to summon a little surprise. As you might expect, their accounts were diametrically opposed to each other. Linus thought a delightful band played at the restaurant. Zelda found the band too noisy and the singer untalented."

"Maybe the truth lies somewhere in-between," mused Grayson.

"Linus thought his burger was perfectly grilled and delicious. Zelda wasn't impressed by her burger whatsoever, although she'd given the staff tons of instructions on how to make it, and probably dire threats if they messed up."

"Not everyone can handle that kind of pressure." Grayson put our meals on plates and took them to the kitchen table.

"Linus thought Quittin' Time was charming," I started.

"Hold it right there. Charming? Quittin' Time?"

I said, "He said he always ate at home, except for one lunch foray to the restaurant. I got the impression that it hadn't been recent. Zelda, of course, rolled her eyes over the restaurant."

"What did the two of them make of each other?" asked Grayson curiously as he sat opposite me at the table.

"Well, that's the interesting part. There seems to be no romantic spark at all. But they're meeting for coffee soon, just to chat."

Grayson asked, "Chat? About what?"

"Right? It doesn't seem as if the two of them would have anything at all to say to each other. But get this—according to Linus, they were talking about everything from neuroscience's effect on the arts to ethics in matters of technology. Oh, and mythology."

Grayson blinked at me. "What?"

"You heard me. What do you make of that?"

Grayson said, "Okay, I was wrong. You *were* able to surprise me. Not so much with Linus. I know how much that man reads. Plus, he reads widely—just about everything he can get his hands on. But Zelda? She always seems completely focused on neighborhood issues and things like that. Don't get me wrong—she's always seemed sharp. But I'd never considered her any kind of intellectual."

"That's where you and I sold Zelda short. Both of her parents were intellectuals, apparently. And then there's the fact that she won trivia night."

Grayson nodded. "You're right. Well, I'm glad she and Linus have made friends. Maybe that will keep Zelda busy and less-inclined to walk around looking for HOA violations."

We dug into the takeout, eating the mouthwatering food as if it were haute cuisine. Fitz sat contentedly in one of the other chairs, washing his face.

"This is the perfect ending for the day," I said, taking a sip of beer. "Tell me how things went at the paper today. I know you said you were going to interview some folks and try to get some good quotes for tomorrow's edition."

Grayson gave me a wry look. "Well, I'd like to say that everybody I talked to gave me tons of information and now the case is closed. But that's not entirely the case."

I smiled at him. "You ran into a few people who didn't want to talk to journalists?"

"*Nobody* wanted to talk to journalists. Not today."

I quirked an eyebrow. "Now, that's unusual. Ordinarily, you have the ability to charm people in every given situation. I've always envied that."

"This was definitely not one of those days where anyone thought I had an iota of charm. I had a lot of doors shut in my face today."

I asked, "Did you have any luck with Paige Lee?"

Grayson made a face. "That was the first door that was closed in my face today. But later, the practice's lawyer gave me a statement on behalf of the clinic this afternoon."

"Really? What did it say?"

Grayson pulled it up on his phone. "*It is with profound sadness that we acknowledge the untimely passing of Kyle Bowman, a valued member of our medical community. Our thoughts and deepest condolences go out to Kyle's family, friends, and all who knew him at this difficult time.*"

"Hmm," I said. "Nothing about the fact that two of the providers at the clinic have recently died? Or that the clinic was cooperating fully with law enforcement as they investigate the circumstances of Kyle's passing?"

Grayson took a sip of beer, then smiled at me. "This is why the clinic should have had you write their statement for them. It probably also would have been good to address safety at the clinic, even though Kyle's death wasn't on the premises."

"I got the impression Dr. Lee was very concerned about the business implications of these murders. She's probably trying to ensure they release as little information as possible."

"Did you speak with her today, then?"

I nodded, swallowing down a bite of some creamy mashed potatoes. "Dr. Lee came over to Kyle's street after reporting he hadn't come into work. I didn't really speak with her, but I was present when Burton was talking to her. This time, she seemed a lot more shaken than she had at Victor's death earlier in the week."

"Do you think she was worried she was in any danger? It's a valid concern, considering she's lost the two other providers at her office."

I said, "I think that was part of it. She talked about security at the office, and Burton is sending a deputy over there to be a presence. But I think it was more than that. Maybe it was the fact that Kyle was so much younger and really just starting out. Regardless, she seemed to be a lot more affected than she'd been before."

"Did you find out anything else from her?" asked Grayson.

"She didn't have any alibi for last night or this morning. She did talk a little about Kyle. She'd seen him last night before he left work. Dr. Lee had taken over the supervisory physician role for his rotation and apparently enjoys doing things a particular way. So they were reviewing the day between the two of them. It sounded like Kyle was impatient to get out of there."

"Did Dr. Lee know why?" asked Grayson.

I shook my head and pushed my plate away, suddenly feeling extremely full. "She didn't seem to know if it was because it had just been a long day and he wanted to get home, or whether he was leaving to meet somebody."

Grayson said, "Considering what happened, it sure seems possible that he planned on meeting someone. Did the police say whether Kyle's door was forced open or whether he let his killer in?"

"No, and I didn't ask. Maybe Burton can fill us in later." I paused. "But you know, Kyle was a pretty fit young guy. It's hard for me to imagine someone being able to force their way into his house and kill him without him putting up some kind of fight. Of course, he'd mentioned the Airbnb he was renting was in poor repair. Maybe the locks weren't working well."

Grayson said, "Or maybe Kyle knew more than he was letting on about Victor's death."

"That's definitely possible. Maybe Kyle figured out who the murderer was and decided to blackmail them. It sounded like he was pretty short on funds—he'd been determined for a long time to make the commute from Charlotte instead of renting a place here. Maybe he looked at it as a way of making extra money."

"Just not the safest way of getting some cash," said Grayson.

I said, "I also spoke with Roger Driscoll today."

"You were busy, especially for your day off."

I said, "It was after I came back from the gym. I did some yardwork in the front yard before I got cleaned up. He was walking past and stopped by to say hi."

Grayson said, "Had he heard about Kyle's murder?"

"No, but he'd heard all the sirens this morning when the police and ambulances descended on Kyle's house. He was curious if I knew what was going on, so I filled him in."

"Did you find out anything interesting from him?" asked Grayson. He pushed his plate away from him, too, apparently just as stuffed as I was.

"Well, he talked a lot about changing his life and trying to do better. He said he didn't believe Joel Burns could be involved in Victor's death."

Grayson asked, "Did he have any new information that made him come to that conclusion?"

"It didn't sound like it. It sounded more like he'd remembered that Joel was a friend: a friend who'd gone through just as many hard times as he had. He was sorry he'd thought Joel could be involved in the murder and was planning on trying to reconnect with him."

"Did Roger say anything about Kyle?" asked Grayson.

"Just that he didn't know him. That he'd never met him." I sighed. "I'm not saying that I found Kyle a particularly likeable person, but I do feel really bad about what happened to him. He was wrapping up med school, getting his rotations knocked out. He was trying hard and had a bright future ahead of him. Then it was just ripped away from him. It's sad."

Grayson nodded. "He wasn't that much younger than we are. It always reminds me how easy it is to take every day for granted." He paused. "And, on that note, how about some pecan pie?" He gave me a boyish grin.

"I was just thinking how stuffed I was," I said, laughing. "How on earth could I fit in pie?"

"Scientifically speaking, your dessert tube hasn't been filled up yet."

I raised an eyebrow. "Scientifically?"

"Well, it *seems* scientific. At least I think I can find room for pecan pie, and I'm stuffed, too."

And somehow, we managed to do just that.

Chapter Sixteen

The next morning, I was up early. It was a day off from work and the sunrise seemed to promise another beautiful day. I fed Fitz, then headed for a shower, opting not to go to the gym or do any further yardwork for the day. Instead, I ate a tremendous breakfast of several scrambled eggs, a berry bowl, and a fluffy biscuit I hadn't been able to resist buying at the bakery on a recent trip.

Fitz seemed to enjoy the slower pace, especially enjoyed it when I headed right back to bed with another book. This one was a P.D. James that had been on my to-be-read list for a while. Fitz delightedly resumed curling up next to me. I played some light pop music on my phone and we spent the next hour happily doing nothing.

When my doorbell rang, Fitz and I both jumped. I gave the cat a quick rub, then walked to the door, looking carefully out the side window before I opened the door. It was a woman I vaguely recognized, although I couldn't place her. She was middle-aged with high cheekbones and blonde hair pulled back in a classic chignon. She wore a crisply ironed white blouse and well-tailored pants. I finally opened the door.

"Can I help you?" I asked.

She gave me something of a tight smile. "I'm Cheryl Sullivan. You're Ann, aren't you?"

Cheryl Sullivan—Victor's widow and Roger Driscoll's ex-wife. "Hi. Yes, I'm Ann. Would you like to come in?"

She hesitated. "I wasn't planning on coming in. But sure, that would be nice."

Cheryl walked inside and into my tiny sitting room, settling on the chintz-covered wicker sofa.

"Can I get you something to drink?" I asked. "Water? Lemonade?"

"Some water would be great, thanks." Cheryl was looking around the small room with interest, taking in the soft earth tones, vintage rug, and the window seat tucked beneath a large window. As in the other rooms, the walls were lined with bookcases, and books were stacked on any available flat surface.

I came back a minute later with a couple of glasses of water. Cheryl took the glass from me and gave me a small smile. At first, I'd thought her expression seemed cold and remote. But now I could tell that she mostly just seemed nervous.

"I'm so sorry about your husband," I said, hoping to put her at ease. "I'm afraid I didn't really know him, but everyone has said such nice things about him."

I saw Cheryl's eyes fill quickly with tears before she looked down, hiding them beneath her long lashes. "Thank you," she said briskly. "It's been a real shock. I was out of town at the beach with a few friends when I heard the news. I've had a very hard time coming to terms with it, probably because I wasn't here. It's been tough to process that he's really gone."

"That's completely understandable," I said. I was still curious what Cheryl, basically a stranger to me, was doing here at the house. I waited, wanting to let her get around to her reason for being here in her own time.

"You've got so many books," she said with a smile, glancing over all the piles of titles. "And you've read them all?"

"Well, most of them. Some of them I've had for a little while and have been *meaning* to read. It's comforting to me to see all the possibilities of what I can read next. Of course, the ones I've read are like old friends to me." I came to a stop. I tended to run my mouth when I was nervous, and for some reason, Cheryl made me uncomfortable. Maybe it was because I couldn't get a read on her. I couldn't imagine her married to rough Roger Driscoll. But I couldn't picture her with Victor, either. It was almost as if she'd created a particular persona for herself. That distance from who she really was and what she appeared to be might be what was tripping me up.

"That must be nice, to have a built-in comfort system in your home," said Cheryl with something of a brittle smile. "I wish I had the same thing." She waited a moment. "You must be wondering why I've come to visit."

I gave her a polite smile.

Cheryl said, "As I mentioned, I've had such a tough time coming to terms with Victor's death. I came back to Whitby as soon as I heard the news, but I still feel as if I'm struggling to access information. The police were so cautious about the details they provided to me. They didn't even tell me how Victor died. I know you were the one who found my husband, and I was hoping you could help fill me in."

If the police wanted to keep how Victor died quiet, I didn't think I should be the one to tell her what had happened. I carefully said, "I'm so sorry. This must be so tough on you. Unfortunately, if the police want to keep that information quiet, I'm thinking it's because they think it'll be useful in helping them solve the case. That's the most important thing, isn't it? Bringing the murderer to justice?"

Cheryl gave me a wry look. "Is it? For days like today, I think the most important thing is to know more and put my mind at ease. To sleep better at night so that I can function better during the day. You have no idea how much makeup I've had to put on to cover up the circles under my eyes."

I hesitated. Sometimes it was better to be kind than wholly accurate. I'd like to relieve Cheryl's mind on Victor's death. The strangulation with the stethoscope had looked awful, but maybe Victor was already unconscious from the heavy medical reference book that lay beside him. I said, "I can tell you I don't believe Victor suffered at all. I think he was taken completely by surprise. He didn't know what was happening."

I heard Cheryl blow out a small breath. She closed her eyes for just a second before turning her gaze on me. "Thank you," she said. Her eyes glistened with unshed tears.

We sat quietly for a few moments, me not wanting to rush Cheryl. There still seemed to be something else on her mind.

Finally, she said slowly, "There was one other reason I wanted to drop by. I hope you won't take any offence at this. I've heard through the grapevine that you've been helping Veronica Carpenter with a particular research project. She's somebody I try to steer clear of—I've found her very intense and angry. I feel sure she must have had something to do with Victor's death. She seems very unstable to me."

I had no idea how Cheryl found out that Veronica and I were researching together. Unless Veronica had been the one to spread the news. After all, privacy was hardly a concern for her; her entire interest was in advocacy and bringing patient advocacy into the spotlight.

Cheryl continued. "I'd like to ask you to discontinue doing research with Veronica. I feel the work she's doing is somehow planned to discredit my husband's memory and the work he's done through the years."

I said gently, "I'm sorry for any pain you're in. I realize you've had to handle a lot. I can tell you, though, that I can't stop helping Veronica. It's part of my job as a reference librarian. And I can assure you that I haven't seen any indication that any part of this project is meant to hurt your husband's legacy in any way. It's the type of work that's meant to be presented at medical conferences and to that type of audience." In other words, very dissimilar from the scathing social media posts Veronica had created earlier.

"Are you sure?" Cheryl asked.

"I can't speak to the entire scope of the research project, but from everything I've seen, it's completely educational in its direction. It's meant to inform healthcare professionals about issues related to patient wellbeing."

Cheryl looked as if she wanted to argue the point a little. But then she slumped, the fire that I'd briefly seen, extinguished. "Got it," she said in a tired voice.

I said, "You believe Veronica was the person who murdered your husband?"

Cheryl gave a weary laugh. "At this point, I'm not sure what I believe. All I know is that she made Victor's life hell for at least the last year. She kept showing up at his office or at our house unannounced. I was trying to convince Victor to file a restraining order on her. I really was. I don't know if I ever thought Veronica would murder somebody, but as soon as I heard the news, she popped immediately into my head."

She set her water glass on the table next to the sofa and stood. "Thank you for being so hospitable. Are you planning on coming to Victor's memorial service? It's at noon at St. John's Methodist. I know it's sort of soon, but I felt I needed to have some closure. I'm not sure having a service will help, but I thought I'd give it a try. I'm going to be heading over there shortly to make sure everything is set up for later."

I didn't have any plans for the afternoon, after all. "I'll be there," I promised.

"Thank you. It'll be good to have a friendly face there. I feel like everyone in town has looked down on me since Victor and I got married. That they've been judging me for leaving Roger."

I said, "I don't think many of them are in the position to judge anybody. Divorce seems just as common here in Whitby as it does everywhere else."

Cheryl nodded, her eyes still looking weary. "Roger and I didn't have the best marriage. I guess we were a sort of odd match to begin with. We had a lot in common at first, but then we grew apart as we got older. 'Tumultuous' would be a good word to describe it." She rubbed her head absently, as if feeling the beginnings of a headache. "Of course, I'll be shocked if Roger shows up at the funeral. He didn't care for Victor, even when we were kids."

Roger had told me he planned on attending Victor's service but I decided not to say anything about it. "They were totally different personalities, I bet," I said instead.

A small smile twisted Cheryl's lips. "That's one way to put it. He was always so jealous of Victor. Everything seemed to come easily to Victor. He came from money, he had a supportive family, he was smart, he was hardworking, he did well in school. Then he ended up as a well-respected professional here in town. Roger couldn't stand any of it."

I said, "Roger moved to my neighborhood, and we had a block party the other night. A group of us were talking, and I got the impression that Roger had always been happy with his job in construction. That he found it personally satisfying."

Cheryl gave a short laugh. "That sounds to me like Roger putting a spin on the truth. Yes, he's good at his job. And he does find it satisfying to a certain degree. But he's so defensive about it, especially around people like Victor. Roger could just be incredibly intense all the time. Brooding. That's why I found Victor so attractive," she added sadly. "He was kind and thoughtful. The polar opposite of Roger."

Cheryl gave me an apologetic smile. "I'm sorry for taking up so much of your time. Thanks again, and I look forward to seeing you at the service. You've really helped me calm down about . . . well, everything. I felt very uncertain this morning when I woke up, and I knew it was going to be tough facing a funeral without having more information going into it."

"I'm happy to help out," I said. "I'll see you in a few hours."

Chapter Seventeen

After Cheryl left, I gave Grayson a call. "Did you know Victor's memorial service is today?"

He said in a teasing voice, "Actually, I printed it in the paper."

I said, "That's just a testament to how distracted I've been lately. Are you planning on going?"

"As a matter of fact, Cheryl Sullivan called me up and asked if I could cover it for the paper, to commemorate it. Want me to run by and pick you up? Maybe at 11: 15? I know that's early, but Victor was such a popular figure in town that I'm guessing it might be hard getting seats at the church."

"See you then," I said.

The methodist church was indeed full. Despite it being a Wednesday afternoon, it seemed as if every patient Victor Sullivan had ever treated was at the church. Grayson and I waited in line to enter the sanctuary and were grateful to find a seat. It was a beautiful old church with stunning stained-glass windows, wooden pews with plush cushions, and a majestic pipe organ in the choir loft. There were flower arrangements everywhere. It felt as if everyone in town must have contributed one. Lilies, carnations, gladioli, and roses covered the front of the church.

Grayson whispered to me, "Look who's here."

Sure enough, true to his word, Roger Driscoll was in the sanctuary, there for his old enemy's memorial service. I said, "He said he wanted to turn over a new leaf. I guess this is his way of starting the process."

The service itself was lovely. Cheryl spoke loving words about Victor for the eulogy, tears glistening in her eyes. According to the program we received at the door, Victor's favorite hymns were played, including "Blessed Assurance," and "How Great Thou Art."

The minister announced that there was a reception in the church hall, so the congregation adjourned the sanctuary. The church hall was a spacious, well-lit room adjacent to the sanctuary with high ceilings and large windows. There were nearly as many flower arrangements in the church hall as there had been in the sanctuary. A long table held finger sandwiches, fruit platters, salads, and an assortment of pastries and desserts.

Cheryl spotted me and came over to greet me. "Thanks again for talking to me this morning, Ann. I'm sorry I just showed up like that."

"It was good to see you this morning, Cheryl. No worries at all." I waved a hand to indicate the reception. "Everything is lovely. The service was just beautiful."

Cheryl smiled at me. "Thanks. I put a lot of time and thought into planning it. Maybe that's because it was a good diversion for me instead of falling apart at home. I figured there would be a lot of people here, and so I felt some pressure to make everything perfect."

"Well, you succeeded," I said. "I'm sure Victor would be pleased."

Cheryl turned to Grayson. "And thanks to you for covering the service and taking photos. I wanted to show that Victor was loved by so many people in town."

"I'm happy to be here," said Grayson. "And I'm sorry again for your loss."

Cheryl stepped away to speak with several people walking our way. I filled plates for Grayson and me while he snapped photos for the paper. I settled at a small table and started eating while Grayson wrapped up.

"Are you saving these seats, Ann?" asked a familiar voice. I looked up to see Joel Burns there.

"Just one of them, for Grayson. Have a seat," I said, motioning to one of the folding chairs. "Good to see you."

He smiled at me. "Thanks. It's not *quite* as awkward being here as I thought it might be. I wavered a little on coming. But I'm really wanting to have a let-bygones-be-bygones mentality."

"That's what Roger Driscoll was telling me recently, too. He thought that was the best way to keep moving forward."

Joel smiled again. "That's really why I'm here. Roger called me for coffee this morning and to catch up. I thought his attitude was contagious."

I glanced around. "I don't see him here at the reception."

"No, he told me he was going to the service, speaking briefly to Cheryl afterwards, and then heading out to run a couple of errands. He gave me a ride over here, though, and is going to pick me up in a few minutes. I lost my license because of a DWI." He shook his head, a look of self-loathing crossing his features. "At least I was just pulled over, and I didn't hurt anyone when I was behind the wheel. I can't believe I was doing that kind of thing. Addiction turned me into a totally different person."

"Sounds like Roger is being a good friend."

Joel said, "He sure is. I'd forgotten all the fun we used to have together in the past. A group of us had poker nights. Roger and I both enjoyed fishing, so we'd hang out at the lake early in the morning and see what we could catch. Roger and Cheryl had great Halloween parties, too. We'd dress up, drink, have a blast." Joel shook his head. "My therapist is encouraging me to find ways to keep doing the things I loved doing, but without alcohol. I've got to reframe the events, she said."

Joel's gaze seemed to freeze as he was glancing around the large room. I turned to see Burton there, keeping an eye on the proceedings with interest. "Everything okay?" I asked.

Joel nodded. "Yeah. At least, I hope so. The police talked to me again yesterday about Kyle Bowman's death. Once again, I was alibi-free, just piddling around the house and applying for jobs."

"How's the job hunt going?" I asked. I remembered that during his panel talk, Joel had mentioned that his addiction issues had led to the loss of his job. As he'd put it, everything in his life had spiraled out of control in every possible direction.

Joel brightened. "Pretty well. I mean, I don't want to jinx it, so maybe I shouldn't say anything. But I've got a second interview for a remote position tomorrow morning. I'm excited about it. Fingers crossed, anyway."

"Hey, that's great!"

Joel said, "I really feel like things are turning around for me. The trick is that I'm showing up. Well, not just showing up . . . I'm helping make the opportunities happen to begin with. Then I'm there for the interviews, with no alcohol or substances in my system."

"That sounds like a real milestone."

"It is, isn't it?" Joel looked pleased. "Finally, things might start going my way. I'm going to make things happen." His gaze wandered over again to Burton. "If I can just get myself out of this murder investigation. Thank goodness it's a remote position, or else being a suspect wouldn't exactly help my chances of getting the job."

I said, "I'm sure it's just a matter of protocol for the police to follow-up with everyone they spoke with after Victor's death."

Joel gave me a sad smile. "Thanks for trying to make me feel better. I just don't see how they can think I have anything to do with Kyle's death. I didn't even know the kid. And, in terms of Victor's death, I hadn't seen or spoken to him for a long time. If anything, I was starting to realize I needed to make amends with Victor. It wasn't all his fault that my marriage ended. I had a lot to do with that, too, even though I wasn't wanting to see it at first. But then, Victor died before I could reach out to him and show him that I'd changed."

"I'm sorry," I said.

Joel took a sip of his coffee and was quiet for a moment. "That's probably one of the biggest regrets I have. That Victor didn't get the chance to see how far I'd come. I'd made it through recovery, now I've got a job prospect. He'd have been cheering me on," he said sadly. "Victor actually did me a huge favor, helping me see I was on the wrong track. The more I've thought about it, I think the reason he told Dena about my affair is that he thought I was going down the wrong road."

"It sounded at the panel that you got some great help, professionally, too. It's good to hear Whitby has good resources here."

Joel said, "It was a surprise and a real blessing. My family told me right away that I needed therapy to deal with my feelings. Nobody had much money, but they all chipped in to get me some help."

We chatted a few more minutes about the different healthcare professionals Joel had worked with. Then talk moved back to the murder investigation. "Have you thought more about who might be responsible for these deaths? I'm guessing the police probably asked you what your thoughts were."

Joel made a face. "They sure did. I'd thought at first that it must be somebody Victor worked with . . . probably Dr. Lee or Kyle. I was clearly totally wrong about Kyle, and I feel awful about that."

"You didn't know," I said. "He sounded like a viable suspect at the time."

"True. But now I feel bad about throwing any kind of suspicion on Dr. Lee, either. I wasn't party to what was going on between Victor and her. Victor had been drinking when he'd talked about her, and I was drinking too, so I'm not exactly the most reliable witness. I'm wondering now if Victor just blew the whole thing out of proportion. Maybe Dr. Lee did something really minor, and Victor made it sound like it was something huge."

Like Dr. Lee taking office supplies home or scrolling through social media on her phone during her lunch break. But I just nodded in response.

Joel said with a sigh, "Anyway, it was just Victor's opinion. And now Victor isn't even here to ask him what he meant by Dr. Lee doing something wrong." He looked around the room again, this time a bit more broodingly. "I keep catching people staring at me out of the corner of my eye. I hope the cops can figure out who's responsible for these murders soon. I know some people think I had something to do with Victor's death."

I looked around, too, but I couldn't see what Joel was talking about. Everyone seemed to be focusing on their lunch, talking to friends, or waiting to speak to Cheryl.

He continued, "I know I've given the whole town a terrible impression of myself for the past year. I've got to set out to reverse that. It hurts me that people have such a poor opinion of me."

I said gently, "People might talk, but they're also pretty quick to forgive and forget."

Joel gave me a grateful smile. "Thanks, Ann. I hope you're right. It all comes down to me and my behavior that made them form the opinion in the first place. My therapist has helped me come to terms with that. I'm not going to blame anyone but myself. I'll prove to everyone that I'm a better person than I used to be."

An older woman at the table next to us glared at Joel. This time, I did see what he was talking about. He gave me a rueful look. "Thanks for letting me sit with you. I'd better talk to Cheryl real quick and then be on my way."

"Good luck with the interview," I said.

He smiled at me and set off.

The older woman was someone I recognized from the library. She had silver-gray hair, neatly styled and held back with a classic barrette. She carried a clutch purse, and the term was very appropriate since she held it close to her as if she suspected someone was going to steal it from her.

She plopped down next to me. "Just wanted to make sure you weren't taken in by that Joel, Ann. He's not someone you need to get involved with."

Small towns could be the worst. "Oh, I'm not involved with him, Mrs. Thompson. He's just an acquaintance." My boyfriend, of course, was still taking pictures around the reception hall. I could point him out as proof, but I wasn't positive that Mrs. Thompson, in her current mood, would even listen to me.

"Joel is one of the biggest fakes I know. He killed Victor. One-hundred percent." She sat back to see my reaction to this explosive news.

She looked irritated to see the doubt I knew was crossing my features. "I'm serious, Ann. I heard a huge argument between Joel and Victor just months before Victor died."

I frowned. "Did you tell the police about this?"

She sniffed. "I don't like dealing with the police. Besides, I don't enjoy getting involved in these things."

Although she was certainly trying to get involved in stopping me from having "a relationship" with Joel. "Did you hear what the argument was about?" I asked.

Mrs. Thompson glowered at me. "Does it really even matter? The point is that Joel was furious with Victor. That's why he killed him. Victor Sullivan was my doctor. Now I have to find another one! It's all most dissatisfying."

"Still, it could help if you told me what you overheard," I said coaxingly.

Mrs. Thompson considered this. Then she grudgingly said, "I suppose so. I heard Joel asking Victor for money. I don't know what he wanted the money for. The point is that he was very unhappy with Victor. Maybe, in the months between when I heard the argument and when he finally killed Victor, he was just boiling over with that rage. That's why he killed him."

"That could be, I suppose," I said. "Thanks for letting me know."

The old woman gave me a tight smile, clutched her purse even tighter to her, and swept off to get more food.

Grayson finally joined me again. "Sorry, that took a while. I also managed to get a few quotes from folks about Victor."

I pushed the plate of food toward him. "That's good. Sounds like you'll have a nice story in the paper tomorrow. Cheryl will really be pleased."

"Yeah, she was happy to have someone from the paper here." He took a big bite of his finger sandwich. "Seems like you had some company, at least, while you were waiting on me."

"Yes," I said, "although I'm still processing it. You probably saw me speaking with Joel for a while. He seemed pretty worried about the police thinking he's a suspect."

"I'm sure that's because he's trying to piece his life together and doesn't need any setbacks," said Grayson.

"True. He talked a lot about trying to turn his life around. Then one of my patrons from the library stopped by the table and told me Joel was a liar and a fake and killed her doctor."

"Whoa!" Grayson said. "That's a lot to lay on you."

"I think she was just mad that she has to find a new doctor," I said with a grin. "She was looking for somebody to blame."

Grayson said, "Sounds like it. Since this is your day off, aren't you about ready to get out of here? I'll finish this up really quickly, and we can head on out. I know you've got other things to do with your day."

"Sure, we can do that. I know you've got work to do on the paper, anyway. Although I have to admit that I don't really have that much to do. I've just got an appointment to snuggle with Fitz and read. That's pretty much it."

"Fitting in a little self-care is probably the most important thing on your list. It's been a tough week."

"You're totally right. The downtime is important and helps me get through the rest of the week." I paused for a moment, looking across the room in surprise.

"What is it?" asked Grayson.

Chapter Eighteen

I didn't even have time to respond before Veronica Carpenter joined us at the table. Although I'd been surprised to see Roger and Joel at the service, I was shocked to see Veronica here. Considering the fact that Cheryl had just asked me that very morning not to help Veronica with her research, I was sure Cheryl wasn't delighted to see her at her husband's memorial service.

"Is it okay if I sit with you, Ann?" she asked with a smile. She sat down before I had a chance to respond.

I introduced Grayson, and she smiled at him. Then she said, "You're probably surprised to see me here. I just wanted to show the police that I have nothing to hide. I figured Burton would probably be here."

I asked, "Have the police been talking with you again?"

"Oh yeah," she said, making a face. "They spoke with me earlier this morning about Kyle. And of course, I didn't have a good alibi for his death, which stinks. I don't know why they'd even think I would murder Kyle, anyway. He wasn't even working at the clinic when my husband was alive."

Grayson said, "It's probably just routine for the police to speak again with everyone they spoke to before."

"Maybe," said Veronica. "It didn't feel that way, though. They kept pressing me, and I couldn't give them any information about Kyle at all. As far as I know, I never even met the guy. But I felt bad for him. There's no way he could have learned much about medicine during that rotation. Not with Victor being his supervising physician."

I could still hear the sour note in her voice when she mentioned Victor. I did think the research and Veronica's focus on advocacy was ultimately going to help her move forward. But it was clear that part of her was still stuck in the past.

Veronica continued, "All the same, I felt terrible for Kyle's parents. They must be devastated. He'd obviously been doing really well in school and had been getting ready for this great profession. Then all of that promise was just gone." A dark look crossed her face. "I know all about that. It's how I felt about my husband's and my future. We had all these plans, these ideas for the kinds of things we'd do together, then they were just gone in a second."

Grayson said, "I'm sorry. That must have been awful."

"It was. But now I'm trying to move forward in a different way. I think my husband would be proud of the work I'm doing to get the word out to doctors." She glanced across the room at Burton, looking brooding. "If the cops would just leave me alone, it would free up more of my time. I've told them several times that I hadn't seen Victor for ages."

I cleared my throat. "Actually, I wanted to talk to you about that. Someone told me you'd argued with Victor recently—shortly before his death. This person I know saw you."

Veronica paled. "You didn't tell the police that?"

"I didn't, but don't you think you should?" I asked. "Get in front of it? Because word always manages to get out. That's what happens in a small town."

Veronica didn't look sure about that. "I just slipped up, Ann. I'd been doing really well, focusing on moving forward instead of dwelling on the past. It's hard, you know. Moving forward isn't a straightforward process. I let my emotions get the better of me, just one more time. That's something I've been working on, but haven't mastered yet." She absently rubbed her forehead as if she was getting a headache. "I'm just worried the police would totally misunderstand that and lock me up."

"No one's locking you up without proof," I said.

"Right. But they'd start digging further into my dealings with Victor, wouldn't they?" She sighed. "I'd come across Victor unexpectedly. I was minding my own business, out running errands. I was deep inside my own thoughts. Victor spoke to me, and I just lost it."

"What did he say?" I asked.

I could see the fury flame in her eyes as she remembered. "He told me he did a lot of good for people and that 'my campaign against him was doing nothing but harm. It wouldn't bring my husband back. I lost it. I said that *I* was doing a lot of good myself and while it wouldn't bring him back, it might help others from ending up in the same situation."

Grayson said, "It sounds like you made a good point."

"Maybe, but I made it in the wrong way. I raised my voice to him. And I'm sure my blood pressure must have shot up like crazy. I backed off. Like I said, though, I'm worried the cops won't see that interaction the same way I do."

I said, "Still, you should tell them about it. They're sure to find it out." I paused. "Have you thought more about who might have been involved in Victor's death?"

"Well, of course, I thought it must be Joel. He just kept cheering me on whenever I wrote something negative about Victor on social media. But it seems like Joel has his life on track now. Grayson, I read your piece in the paper on him—how he'd overcome his addiction and was trying to move forward in a positive way. I have a lot to learn from Joel and his experiences. So now, I'm thinking it's got to be Paige Lee."

"Victor's coworker," I said.

Veronica nodded. "It makes sense, doesn't it? After all, two people from the clinic have died now, and both of the deaths were murders. Who else was that close to both of them? Maybe she wanted to have the whole clinic to herself or something." She hesitated. "The only thing that gives me pause is that Dr. Lee always seemed really cold and unemotional, though. It's tough for me to picture her as a killer. But I can't think who else could have done it. That's what I told the police when they spoke to me this morning."

I thought again about Victor telling Joel that Paige Lee had been doing something she shouldn't have done.

Veronica said, "Are you going to be at the library this afternoon, Ann? I thought you could help me find some more resources to explore."

"Actually, I've got the day off today. But I'll be back in the library tomorrow morning."

Veronica said, "Is there a time that would work better for you? Do you have anything else scheduled?"

"Any time would be fine, but it's probably quieter earlier in the morning. I'd think there wouldn't be much happening on a Thursday morning. I don't even think there are any storytimes tomorrow morning."

Veronica said, "I'll be there bright and early then. Thanks."

I looked over at Grayson, and he must have read my mind. He took a last bite of his food, then said, "Well, we'd better get going. I've got to get back to the office. Good to meet you, Veronica."

As we walked away, I said, "Thanks for rescuing me. Sometimes I feel like I don't have a lot of boundaries between my work and my personal life. I've even had people hand me their library books to return to the library for them when they see me out in public."

Grayson snorted. "That's crazy."

"I know. I had the sudden feeling Veronica was going to whip out her phone and get me to research stuff right there at the funeral reception."

We got into Grayson's car. He said, "So who have we got left on our suspect list? Kyle obviously isn't a contender anymore, unless we're talking about two separate murderers. Which I guess we could be."

"I'm not sure it's as complex as all that. I'm wondering if it's all really simple and we're just not seeing it." I thought for a few moments. "I feel like there's something I heard today that should stick out. Something important. But I can't put my finger on what it is." I shrugged. "Anyway, going back to your question. We have Roger Driscoll, first of all."

Grayson said, "Right. Our new neighbor. Welcome to the neighborhood . . . we suspect you of murder."

I grinned at him. "When you put it like that, it sounds pretty bad. But he has plenty of motive. He had a poor relationship with Victor when he was living next door to him. Then things really deteriorated when Victor and Roger's wife started an affair and eventually got married."

"That would sour anybody," said Grayson.

"For sure. But now, he seems determined to turn his life around. He's been working hard on rediscovering old friendships and trying to move forward."

Grayson said, "Then we have Joel Burns, who's trying to do the same thing."

"Exactly. Joel lost his marriage and spiraled into addiction. He used to blame Victor for a lot of that, although he seems like he's shouldering a lot more of the blame now. Victor told Joel's wife that Joel was having an affair."

Grayson said, "I'm still not sure why Victor did that."

"It sounds like Joel now believes Victor thought that was the ethical thing to do. That Victor wouldn't have been able to handle hanging out with Joel and his wife and pretending Joel hadn't cheated on her."

Grayson said, "So Joel's wife left him, he started grappling with addiction, and he lost his job."

"He lost his driver's license too. Joel told me that today. He said Roger was driving him back and forth to the service."

Grayson said, "Then we've got your patron, Veronica Carpenter. It sounded like she'd been lying about when she'd last seen Victor."

"That's right. She looked terrified when I mentioned a witness had seen her yelling at Victor not long before his death."

"Zelda," said Grayson with a smile. "Quite a witness."

"Zelda. To her credit, Veronica admitted to it right away when I brought it up."

Grayson said, "Yeah, but I'm not so sure she's planning to tell the police about it. She's got a lot of pent-up emotion—I can totally see her lashing out at Victor. Hitting him over the head with a textbook and then strangling him? It could happen."

"I know. She and her husband were apparently really close. Like she said, she had her entire future planned, and then it was taken away from her prematurely."

"By illness," said Grayson. "Not murder."

"True, but in Veronica's mind, her husband's cancer should never have progressed to the point it did. Victor should have run those tests he was reluctant to run. He should have listened more carefully when her husband described his symptoms. It's ironic that a doctor who's been praised for being a listener ended up ignoring what one of his patients was telling him."

Grayson said, "It does. But then Victor is starting to sound like he might have been a man of contradictions. So then we have Paige Lee."

"Yes. From everything I've heard, he and Dr. Lee had a pretty contentious relationship. They'd dated for a little while, which hadn't gone well. It sounds like Victor was hard on Dr. Lee, like he was on all of his staff. Burton mentioned Victor had been upset when Dr. Lee brought office supplies home and was unhappy when she'd spent time on her phone between patients."

Grayson said, "Sort of nitpicking her to death."

"Exactly. At any rate, there is definitely no love lost there. Plus, Victor told Joel that Dr. Lee had been doing some sort of untoward thing. He was vague about it, so we don't know if it has anything to do with the petty stuff like the office supplies, or something more major."

Grayson said, "That's quite a group of suspects."

"Do you have one you think might be responsible yet?" I asked.

Grayson pulled the car into my driveway, then mulled over the question for a moment. "You know, I'm not sure. I'm thinking, after seeing Veronica at the service, that maybe she fits the bill pretty well. Of course, that could be because she got caught out in a lie right in front of me. Who is your pick?"

I said slowly, "I'm not totally sure. I wish I could remember what stood out to me today when I was talking to different people."

"It'll come to you. Okay, take some time off. Take care of yourself." He reached out and gave me a hug.

I clung to him for a second, enjoying his warm steadiness. "Thanks. I'll talk to you later."

Chapter Nineteen

It ended up being good that I'd taken Grayson's advice and taken the rest of Wednesday easy because Thursday morning started off with a bang. I knocked my coffee over and it went splashing all over the kitchen, just barely missing hitting poor Fitz. I realized I hadn't put my cell phone on the charger the night before, and the battery was completely dead. Then I couldn't find my keys when it was time for me to leave for the library.

"It's like the universe is telling me not to go to work today," I said to Fitz.

His solemn face seemed to agree with me.

After five minutes of searching for the lost keys, I found them buried at the very bottom of my purse. "I'm not usually so scatterbrained," I muttered. I bundled Fitz into his carrier and got to the library without further mishap. It was lucky I hadn't been tasked with opening up for the day.

Although I'd told Veronica at the service that it was unlikely to be busy on a Thursday morning, I was quickly proven wrong as soon as I walked through the doors. Luna was on the floor in front of the circulation desk with a hand vac. She grimaced at me as I went in. "Glitter," she said pithily.

"Did one of the moms drop it?" I asked. "I thought we didn't have any storytimes or craft workshops today."

"Even worse," said Luna with a snort. "*I* dropped it. Things haven't been going right for me since I woke up this morning."

"You and me both," I said. "I was apparently torn between destroying my house and losing everything except my head. Maybe things will go better here at work."

"Yeah, as long as you don't throw glitter all over the library like I did. But it doesn't seem to be starting off on a good foot. The copier is possessed."

I groaned. There was nothing worse at the library than dealing with the copier. The printer was also pretty awful, but the copier was in a class by itself. It jammed, smudged ink, skipped pages or fed multiple pages at once, threw up error codes, and experienced network connectivity issues. In short, the thing was a disaster. I'd recently put a sign up on the copier instructing patrons not to kick it. It might sound like an unnecessary sign, but it definitely wasn't. Patron kicks had also resulted in malfunctions over the years.

"I better go see what's going on," I said glumly. "What have you heard? What's the issue with it?"

Luna said, "It's producing copies with a green tint or hue of some kind. One patron told me it was possessed by aliens."

"Seems likely." I squared my shoulders and headed off toward the copier. Before I could get there, though, Veronica Carpenter walked in through the sliding doors. Although I hadn't been looking forward to working with her, her timely arrival before I had to tinker with the errant copier was perfect.

"Is now a good time?" she asked. She seemed distracted, though, and was already heading for a table in the group study area before I could answer her.

I said, "Is everything going okay?"

Veronica gave a short laugh. "It sounds like you can tell I'm a little out of whack this morning."

I said dryly, "It seems to be contagious. Let's just say that you're not the only one."

Veronica pulled out her laptop and a notebook from her laptop bag. "After I got back from Victor's service yesterday, I took a brief detour from my usual research. You know how I was talking about Paige Lee." She dropped her voice even though there was no one around us.

I nodded. "You were thinking she was the most likely candidate for the murders, since she was now the only provider left at the clinic."

"That's right. It just seemed really coincidental to me." Veronica shrugged. "I'll feel dumb if she ends up being murdered today, but right now, she seems like the only person who makes sense for having committed the crimes. Anyway, I got to thinking about how another former patient of the clinic reached out to me online. She said she'd been reading my social media posts about Victor's malpractice and the other problems at the clinic. She wanted to add that the office had over-billed her."

"She was one of Victor's patients?" I asked.

"No, she was one of Paige Lee's. Out of interest, I stayed up last night and tried to see what else I could find. I looked online for any other patients who might have complained about over-billing." Veronica pulled her laptop closer and started typing on it.

I could tell the direction she was going in. The only problem was that complaints about over-billing were rampant. I'd assisted a couple of patrons before with hospital bills and office bills.

Veronica must have known what I was thinking. She said, "I was sure almost every patient thinks they're being over-billed. That was confirmed when I found a few mentions on social media about the clinic and unhappy patients talking about their bills in online reviews for the practice."

"But nothing that struck you as particularly egregious?" I asked.

"Well, I just wasn't sure. Yeah, there were exorbitant bills. But medical costs here in the US are often exorbitant, anyway. So I looked up malpractice suits. I'm surprised I didn't think of doing that before. I filed one against Victor, after all. I should have thought about the fact that other people might have done the same."

I said, "I guess the reason we didn't look that up is because you were trying to move in a different direction with the research. We were looking up data you could use at conferences to persuade providers to be better at listening to patient symptoms."

"That's correct. I was trying to cast the net wider, for sure. And move forward at the same time, instead of focusing only on that one clinic and the problems there."

I asked, "What did you find out when you looked for suits?"

Veronica turned her laptop around. "It turns out that over-billing and fraudulent practices can sometimes be a component of malpractice claims." She pointed to some of the information on the screen. "Mostly where the over-billing leads to a patient receiving unnecessary treatments or procedures, which lead to complications. And I found there were a couple of suits involving Paige Lee."

"Not Victor Sullivan?"

Veronica shook her head. "Not this time."

I looked at the names and the information Veronica had typed up. Then I turned to her. "You met my friend Grayson yesterday. He's the editor of the local paper. Would it be okay if I shared this information with him? He might be up for doing an investigative report."

Veronica quickly agreed. "That would be perfect. I'd be totally up for researching this myself, but I'm trying to stay focused on the big picture and honing the talk I'll be giving."

"Of course. Did you want to work on that today?"

Veronica shook her head again. "I was planning to. But I ended up staying awake most of the night last night, between looking up this stuff on Paige Lee and then thinking about it all. Do you think this billing issue could be connected to what happened?"

I did, of course. It sounded likely that this possibly fraudulent activity was what Victor had been alluding to when he said Dr. Lee was up to something she shouldn't be doing. If Victor had been angry with Dr. Lee about office supplies, I could only imagine what he'd do if he discovered over-billing or fraud of any kind. "It's possible," I said.

Veronica took this and ran with it. "Maybe Victor told Dr. Lee that he was going to tell the police what he suspected unless she turned herself in. That would definitely have been a motive for her to kill him."

I said cautiously, "That's true, but we need to proceed carefully with this. It could be harmful for us to make allegations that aren't true. If they *are* true, the situation could be dangerous for us."

Veronica nodded solemnly. "That's a good point. And right now, I'm pretty risk-adverse. I've been reminded that life is short, and I'd rather not cut mine any shorter than it's supposed to be."

"Besides telling Grayson, I'll also notify the police. It's something they should know, even if it ends up not being relevant."

Veronica said, "That's totally fine. They should know what's going on. Do you want me to email you the information I've found?"

"That would be great, if you could." So Veronica sent the information right over, then put her laptop away. "I'm going to head back home and take it easy the rest of the morning. Thanks for your help, Ann."

I gave her a distracted smile, and she set off for the door.

A few minutes later, I was on the phone with Grayson. I filled him in on what Veronica had discovered, and he gave a low whistle. "Now, that's what I call a motive."

"Right? I'm not sure if Dr. Lee is the one who murdered Victor, but it seems like she might have had good reason to." I glanced up as five or six people walked into the library. "Things are picking up now, so I'm not going to be able to help research with you, unfortunately. But malpractice suits are usually a matter of public record."

"Civil court records, I'm guessing?" asked Grayson.

"That's right. Or you can check the North Carolina Medical Boards. They should maintain public records of suits against providers. Of course, you can also check out Westlaw, LexisNexis, and PACER. Have you got subscriptions to those databases?"

Grayson chuckled. "I think you have an exaggerated opinion of the amount of money the newspaper has in its account."

"Got it," I said, smiling. "Well, if you want to access any of those, let me know. The library has subscriptions to some of them. Oh, and could you call Burton and fill him in for me? I think I'm going to be stuck for a while. It's getting busy in here, plus I have a misbehaving copier to straighten out."

"Will do," said Grayson. "Good luck with everything."

Chapter Twenty

I needed every bit of luck I could muster. The copier flat-out refused to cooperate, choosing instead to shut itself down in a huff. I had to call our repair guy to come out and take care of it. Not having a working copier at the library qualified as a full-fledged disaster. Patrons were groaning over the issue until it finally got fixed a couple of hours later.

That afternoon, Joel Burns came into the library. He spotted me at the reference desk and came over to say hi.

"How are things going, Joel? Did the second interview go well for you?"

Joel said, "Well, I thought it did. But I haven't heard from the company yet."

"Did they tell you when they'd give you an answer?"

He shook his head. "Nope. And I didn't want to ask, because I didn't want to seem pushy. But I decided I should hedge my bets, you know? I'm going to use one of your computers to do some more job searching. That way, even if this job doesn't come through, maybe I'll have something else lined up."

I said, "Sure thing." I pulled out the notebook where we registered a computer to a patron for a specific length of time and jotted his name down. I hesitated. "I know you were talking about remote work. You have a computer at home, don't you?"

"I do . . . don't worry about that. But my internet has been sort of wonky today, so I figured coming into the library would make better sense."

I paused again, not wanting to accuse Joel of anything, but thinking again about what my patron had said at the service, about Joel's argument with Victor. "Joel, there's been something on my mind. Would you be upset if I asked you about something?"

"No, go ahead. Shoot."

I took a deep breath. "It's just that someone told me you and Victor had an argument somewhat recently. And, apparently, somewhat publicly. I know you told me you hadn't seen Victor in a while, so I wanted to get a little clarity on what happened."

Joel gave me a grateful look. "I'm glad you asked. Everybody else in this town just seems to talk dirt about me without asking me in person. I wouldn't want you to have a poor opinion of me."

"It's not true then?" I asked, feeling somehow relieved. I genuinely liked Joel and admired him for his resilience.

Joel said, "I'm afraid that it *is* true, Ann. I'm sorry I didn't tell you the whole truth. I think part of me has been terrified of the police connecting me with Victor's death somehow. I had nothing to do with it, but I still feel like I could somehow get arrested. I already feel like I've hit rock-bottom, but maybe there's further for me to drop."

"I doubt that," I said. "What happened between you and Victor?"

"I know the day your patron is talking about. I was still trying to get back on my feet again. I approached Victor as part of my twelve steps to recovery. I wanted to apologize to him for my treatment of him."

I said, "And Victor didn't accept your apology?"

"He did accept it, actually. But in a moment of weakness, I asked Victor for money. Specifically, I needed it to pay some of my medical bills. I figured if anybody understood about medical bills, it would be Victor." Joel gave a twisted smile. "But Victor turned me right down. He said that he would feel like an enabler if he gave me money because he was sure I'd use it for alcohol or drugs."

I closed my eyes briefly. "Sorry about that, Joel. That must have been very hurtful."

"It was. And maybe because I was tired of feeling pain, I felt anger again. Anger, which was my usual standby emotion. Anger can seem easier to deal with than pain, but it's a lot more corrosive. Anyway, that day I just erupted. I was yelling at Victor, awful things. But, again, something good ended up coming out of it. The incident prompted me to join an anger management program. They've been great at helping me keep my emotions in check."

"Did you end up finding the money for your medical bills?" I asked.

He nodded. "Good old crowdfunding. At any rate, I'm not in any debt."

I said, "Well, I hope one of these jobs comes through soon, Joel."

He smiled at me. "Me too." Then he headed off for the computers to continue his job hunting.

That afternoon, there was just as much chaos as you'd expect, following a morning like that. I was working on research when my computer froze, resulting in missing work. A well-meaning patron attempted to re-shelve all the books he'd pulled out, but somehow managed to put them in the fiction stacks instead of nonfiction. A group of overly-energetic children with their rather lax moms turned the quiet area into a playground until I ushered them back to the children's department. The only good thing was Fitz, who was especially loving. He must have suspected I was in dire need of stress relief.

I wasn't sorry when five o'clock rolled around, my scheduled shift-end for the day. I decided spending time outside would reset me. I changed into junky clothes and focused on yardwork in the backyard this time. The boxwoods definitely needed some attention, and I'd been meaning to give them a haircut. Fitz watched me with interest from a window as I used my hand-held, rechargeable hedge trimmer to make the bushes as neat as I could, then I raked up the debris and put some of it as mulch under other plants, and some in my compost pile.

Then I remembered I'd promised to divide the daylilies and give some to Roger. I moved to the front yard, this time grabbing a small shovel and a trowel. We'd had rain the night before, so the task was much easier than it might have been. Soon I had ten plants to give to Roger. I set them in a grocery bag and headed down the street. I figured I'd just leave the plants outside Roger's house if he wasn't at home.

His car was in the driveway when I got there, so it looked like he might not be out. I tapped lightly on the door. When Roger didn't immediately open the door, I stooped to leave the plants outside his front door. But then he finally appeared.

"Ann," he said with some surprise. Then he saw the bag of daylilies and looked pleased. "Hey, that's great. I'd forgotten we were talking about that."

"I was getting some yardwork done and got the daylilies divided while I had my yard clothes on." I was about to say more when my latent allergies decided to suddenly switch into full gear. I started coughing and sneezing so much that I wondered if Roger would shut the door in my face for his own self-preservation.

Instead, though, he ushered me inside. "Let me get you some water," he said.

I nodded, unable to speak with the coughing. I glanced around the small front room for a place to sit down. It looked as if Roger wasn't much of a housekeeper. Roger's laundry had migrated into the living room and it was hard to tell which was a clean or dirty pile. Although I knew he'd moved in at least a few months ago, he still had boxes with various knick-knacks, pictures, and lamps shoved into them.

Then, I saw something that made me freeze.

Chapter Twenty-One

There was a box that had different holiday decorations spewing out of it. Christmas and Halloween together. I suddenly remembered Joel telling me about the great Halloween parties Roger and Cheryl used to throw before Victor and Cheryl ended up together. And there I could see what looked like a brown delivery uniform, meant to look like a UPS uniform. Burton had said a witness noticed a delivery person in the area the morning of Victor's death.

"Have some water," said Roger, returning with a glass. He froze too as soon as he saw my face. "Everything okay?" He followed my gaze and saw what I was looking at. Then he turned back around, his brows knit together.

I was still coughing too much to get words out, but Roger was no longer offering me the water. I motioned to the door and started heading in that direction. Roger blocked me. He said, "Let's talk for a moment."

I pointed at myself, indicating that talking was one thing I was *not* going to be able to do. I tried to sidestep Roger, but he leaped right back in front of me again. He reached out to grab my arm, dropping the glass in the process.

There was a sudden, peremptory knock at the screen door. "Roger? Roger? I know you're in there."

I had never been so happy to hear Zelda's voice before.

"I need to speak with you about your tremendous mailbox. You didn't install the same type and size mailbox that the rest of the neighborhood has. It's an affront to the area's image," she said crisply. "As well, I'm not fond of your yard décor."

"I'm busy right now," he called out loudly. "Come back later."

Zelda's nosiness finally worked in my favor. "Who's there with you? What are you doing?" she asked suspiciously.

Roger turned to better get rid of Zelda, and I used the opportunity to push past him and through the screen door, nearly knocking down Zelda in the process and still coughing up a storm.

Zelda took one look at my shaken face and Roger's furious one, whipped out a hot pink pepper spray container, and sprayed Roger within an inch of his life, yelling at me to run.

I grabbed Zelda's arm to drag her with me. She flung the pepper spray can at Roger and stumbled to keep up with me as I took off down the street to my house. I shoved Zelda inside and locked the door behind us. Then I checked to make sure the back door was locked, too.

"Get some water for that cough," commanded Zelda as she pulled her phone out. She must have had Burton on speed dial, because she put the call through immediately. "Roger Driscoll just tried to kill Ann," she barked into the phone, although she'd really seen no evidence of that. "He was at his house when we left."

I drank a glass of water, then blew my nose while Zelda watched me critically. "Did he try to poison you?" she demanded. "Is that why you're coughing so much?"

I shook my head and, finally able to speak, said, "No, I just had an allergy attack when I was there. But I saw evidence that Roger was the killer."

Zelda gave me a grim look. "No wonder. You could tell he wasn't a good guy, just from the mess outside his house."

I didn't agree with this statement whatsoever, but would have accepted anything Zelda said at that moment in time.

Sirens roared past my house, startling Fitz, who was used to a very peaceful street. Zelda's face held a certain dour satisfaction. "Go get him," she muttered to the police cars.

I motioned to the sofa. "Want to take a seat, Zelda? I'm definitely taking one. Can I get you something to drink or eat before I do?"

Zelda shook her head. "Nope. Had a snack before I went to Roger's."

"And you're not thirsty? We did run down the street."

Zelda gave a raspy chuckle. "Yes, we did. I didn't think I had it in me."

"You sure did. We bolted down that street," I said, a smile curling at my lips. It was just days ago when I'd told Grayson that Zelda's smoker's cough worried me. But she ran just as capably as I had, and I'd been the one coughing.

We both sat down in the living room, listening as more sirens came and went. My phone rang.

"Grayson," I said.

He answered, "Is everything going okay there? I was leaving work, and it looked like a ton of police cars were heading to our neighborhood."

"I'm fine. But Roger Driscoll is the murderer." I glanced over at Zelda and gave her a smile. "And Zelda just helped me out of a very tricky situation."

"I'll be right there," he said, his voice serious.

And he was. He came in, got Zelda and me something to eat and drink, despite our protestations, and sat in one of the rickety armchairs to hear what we had to say.

Before I could start, though, Burton tapped on the front door. Grayson let him in.

Burton gave me an appraising look, as if trying to make sure I was okay. "You all right, Ann?" he asked gruffly.

"Thanks to Zelda and her pepper spray," I said.

Burton chuckled. "Yeah, I could tell he'd been sprayed. You'll be glad to hear Roger complained of his skin and eyes burning and was crying like a baby from the spray. Lots of respiratory distress, too," he said with a certain amount of grim satisfaction.

Zelda looked especially pleased to hear this.

"So, you got him?" I asked, feeling a tremendous sense of relief wash over me.

"We got him," said Burton with a nod. "He was on the run, but didn't get too far, considering the pepper spray."

Grayson said, "Was he *physically* running, or was he in his car?"

"In his car. But he ran his car into a ditch because he couldn't see with his eyes tearing up. It wasn't much of a chase," said Burton. "But now, if Zelda and Ann could fill me in on what happened. That would be most helpful. I'll get the two of you to sign statements at the station later on."

Zelda shrugged. "I don't know what happened. I just showed up and pepper sprayed the guy because Ann tore out of the house looking like the devil was after her."

Grayson reached out and held my hand.

I said, "Yeah, that's about the way it was. I'd spoken to Roger on Tuesday when he was passing by my house. I was doing yard-work in my front yard, and we got to talking about the different flowers he had at his house. He was interested in getting some of my daylilies, which I needed to divide, anyway." I stopped and took a deep breath, the events of the evening suddenly catching up with me again.

Grayson gave my hand another squeeze. Burton said, "Take your time, Ann. I'm not going anywhere."

After a few moments of deep breathing, I felt better. "Okay. So, after work, I divided up the daylilies and brought them over to Roger's house. My allergies have been bothering me lately. I guess I've been busy or at least, I've put off going to see the doctor about them. I started coughing and sneezing like crazy, and he let me come inside so he could get me some water."

Burton quirked a brow. "Sounds like that little bit of hospitality cost him."

I nodded. "Right. Because while I was waiting for the water, I was just sort of glancing around. The inside was messy, but I figured when you had a guy living alone, that kind of thing can happen."

Zelda gave a sniff as if saying it was something that should *never* happen, under any circumstances. I had never been in Zelda's house, but I had the feeling that it was likely neat as a pin.

"One of the things I noticed when I was looking around was a box of unpacked holiday decorations. Everything was crammed in there, but one thing I noticed was a brown uniform—the type a UPS driver might wear."

Grayson's eyes widened. "The delivery person the witness mentioned seeing at Victor's clinic."

Burton nodded. "That's right. Roger had grabbed the uniform and thrown it in the car with him when he fled. I guess he was planning to take it away and throw it in the lake or destroy it somehow." He looked at me through narrowed eyes. "So Roger came back with the water and could tell you'd seen the uniform. And it was something that *meant* something to you—it wasn't just a costume."

"He sure could. I remembered, too, that Joel had told me recently that Roger used to have these big Halloween parties when they were closer friends. It all started clicking together. So I tried to leave, Roger tried to stop me, and Zelda came over at just the right time to fuss at Roger for an HOA violation."

Zelda sniffed again. "His mailbox and yard décor are disgraces."

Grayson and I tried to hide our smiles. I added, "Zelda sprayed him and we ran here and locked the doors."

"And I called you," said Zelda, preening over her important role in the evening's events.

"Well, it was the breakthrough we needed," said Burton. "I'm sure Roger's prints will end up matching some partials we found at the scene of Victor's death. That delivery uniform and his behavior this evening are also key." He turned to me. "Give me a quick run-through of what you think happened. Why Roger committed two murders."

I said, "Well, I guess the biggest reason the whole thing kicked off is because Roger thought Victor had messed up his life. He lost his wife when Victor started seeing her. He ended up losing his house, which Roger loved." I paused, thinking it through. "Of course, Roger would have known Victor's work schedule after having been his neighbor for so many years. Roger had an old Halloween costume of a UPS deliveryman, and he used it to wait for Victor without gaining too much attention."

"But he didn't bring a weapon with him?" asked Grayson.

"Maybe he did," I said. "Maybe he planned to use a knife or some other weapon that wouldn't be noisy and attract a lot of attention. But when he saw Victor was lugging in a heavy medical textbook, he must have used the element of surprise to grab the book and hit him over the head with it. Then he used the stethoscope Victor wore to finish him off."

Burton nodded. "It was an angry crime. And no matter what Roger was saying about turning over a new leaf, he was an angry guy."

"Exactly. I think he must have been brooding on it all the time. Even though the divorce had happened the previous year, the more he thought about it, the more upset he became."

Zelda piped up. "He was drinking too much at the block party." Her face was a study in censure.

Burton said, "We'd also found out that Victor had been spreading talk about Roger's marriage with Cheryl. Cheryl keeps her private life to herself, but apparently Victor said that Roger's marriage to Cheryl wasn't as happy as Roger was always making out."

"Well, we knew it couldn't have been perfect or Cheryl wouldn't have left Roger for Victor," I said.

"Exactly. But I guess Victor was taking things a step further. I'm wondering if maybe this pushed Roger over the edge. Plus, folks had mentioned Victor and Cheryl were at a local Friday night high school football game recently. They mentioned Roger left early, upset at seeing the two of them there. It had been something he and Cheryl used to do together as inexpensive entertainment when they were married."

I said slowly, "So Roger might have been boiling right below the surface."

Grayson asked, "What about Kyle? Was he somebody who was just in the wrong place at the wrong time?"

I said, "Kyle must have seen something. We'd been hearing that Kyle was always really early at the office. According to Kyle, he'd been delayed the morning Victor died by kitchen equipment malfunctioning. But maybe he was there. Maybe he spotted Roger dressed in the UPS costume."

"Did Kyle know Roger?" asked Grayson.

"He probably didn't, considering Kyle had only just recently moved to town. Or maybe he knew who he was because Victor mentioned him. It could even have happened that Kyle ran into Roger sometime after the murder and recognized him as the delivery man. Kyle had mentioned being short on money," I said.

"Blackmail," said Burton grimly.

Zelda made a disgusted sound. I was sure her primary concern was that Roger was giving the neighborhood a black mark.

"That's what I think. Kyle saw Roger, maybe decided he could make a little money from him, and gave blackmail a go."

Burton said, "But Roger decided he didn't want to pay up, went to Kyle's house, and killed him."

I nodded. "That's what it sounds like."

Burton stood up, stretching a little. "Well, I'm sorry you had to go through all that, Ann, but I sure am glad this case is wrapped up. We've got our physical evidence and your testimony. We can finally put this case to bed."

"You mentioned you needed Zelda and me to come downtown and sign statements?"

Burton nodded. "Tomorrow morning will be fine. We already have plenty to hold Roger overnight. Resisting arrest and assaulting a police officer are just a couple of reasons. Don't worry—the officer's fine. All in a day's work."

With that, he headed for the door. Burton turned around before he walked out. "Before I go, could I speak to you for just a second, Ann?"

I followed him outside. He said, "Sorry about being mysterious. I just didn't want to say anything in front of Zelda. Grayson already knows."

"Knows about what?" I asked.

"He knows about the potential fraud case against Paige Lee," said Burton. "Grayson was the one who filled me in on it earlier today. Anyway, I took a preliminary look at what was going on. I couldn't spend much time on it because of the murder investigations. But it sure looks like she's going to have to answer some tough questions soon." He tipped an imaginary hat to me. "Thanks for your help with that."

"It was really my patron. I'm glad you're looking into it."

I walked back inside to hear Grayson giving Zelda a lively rendition of a typical day at the newspaper office. I wasn't sure if he had just decided to regale her with the story, or if she'd tried to make conversation with him. At any rate, she looked relieved at my return.

Zelda grated, "I don't know about you two, but I could use a drink."

"You've earned any kind of drink you want," I said fervently. "I might have a meager supply of alcohol, but I have a nice variety."

Zelda decided on a bourbon and coke, Grayson favored the light beer, and I had a glass of chardonnay. In this most unlikely of trios, I felt, oddly, at ease. I turned on some relaxing music. Zelda appeared to be reflecting on whatever was going through her mind; likely ill will against Roger Driscoll.

Grayson raised his beer in a toast. "To unlikely alliances and surviving the chaos today."

Zelda and I raised our glasses with a smile.

About the Author

Elizabeth writes the Southern Quilting mysteries and Memphis Barbeque mysteries for Penguin Random House and the Myrtle Clover series for Midnight Ink and independently. She blogs at ElizabethSpannCraig.com/blog, named by Writer's Digest as one of the 101 Best Websites for Writers. Elizabeth makes her home in Matthews, North Carolina, with her husband. She's the mother of two.

Sign up for Elizabeth's free newsletter to stay updated on releases:

https://bit.ly/2xZUXqO

This and That

I love hearing from my readers. You can find me on Facebook as Elizabeth Spann Craig Author, on Twitter as elizabethscraig, on my website at elizabethspanncraig.com, and by email at elizabethspanncraig@gmail.com.

Thanks so much for reading my book...I appreciate it. If you enjoyed the story, would you please leave a short review on the site where you purchased it? Just a few words would be great. Not only do I feel encouraged reading them, but they also help other readers discover my books. Thank you!

Did you know my books are available in print and ebook formats? Most of the Myrtle Clover series is available in audio and some of the Southern Quilting mysteries are. Find the audiobooks here: https://elizabethspanncraig.com/audio/

Please follow me on BookBub for my reading recommendations and release notifications.

I'd also like to thank some folks who helped me put this book together. Thanks to my cover designer, Karri Klawiter, for her awesome covers. Thanks to my editor, Judy Beatty for her help. Thanks to beta readers Rebecca Wahr, Cassie Kelley, and Dan Harris for all of their helpful suggestions and careful reading. Thanks to my ARC readers for helping to spread the word. Thanks, as always, to my family and readers.

Other Works by Elizabeth

Myrtle Clover Series in Order (be sure to look for the Myrtle series in audio, ebook, and print):

Pretty is as Pretty Dies

Progressive Dinner Deadly

A Dyeing Shame

A Body in the Backyard

Death at a Drop-In

A Body at Book Club

Death Pays a Visit

A Body at Bunco

Murder on Opening Night

Cruising for Murder

Cooking is Murder

A Body in the Trunk

Cleaning is Murder

Edit to Death

Hushed Up

A Body in the Attic

Murder on the Ballot

Death of a Suitor

A Dash of Murder
Death at a Diner
A Myrtle Clover Christmas
Murder at a Yard Sale
Doom and Bloom
Southern Quilting Mysteries in Order:
Quilt or Innocence
Knot What it Seams
Quilt Trip
Shear Trouble
Tying the Knot
Patch of Trouble
Fall to Pieces
Rest in Pieces
On Pins and Needles
Fit to be Tied
Embroidering the Truth
Knot a Clue
Quilt-Ridden
Needled to Death
A Notion to Murder
Crosspatch
Behind the Seams
Quilt Complex
The Village Library Mysteries in Order (Debuting 2019):
Checked Out
Overdue
Borrowed Time

Hush-Hush

Where There's a Will

Frictional Characters

Spine Tingling

A Novel Idea

End of Story

Booked Up

Memphis Barbeque Mysteries in Order (Written as Riley Adams):

Delicious and Suspicious

Finger Lickin' Dead

Hickory Smoked Homicide

Rubbed Out

And a standalone "cozy zombie" novel: Race to Refuge, written as Liz Craig